The Redacted Sherlock Holmes Volume VIII

By

Orlando Pearson

Paperback ISBN 978-1-80424-492-0
ePub ISBN 978-1-80424-493-7
PDF ISBN 978-1-80424-494-4

Published by MX Publishing
335 Princess Park Manor, Royal Drive,
London, N11 3GX
www.mxpublishing.co.uk

Cover design Awan

Contents

Some Parisian Hot-Desking

And so what of Professor Moriarty?

Followers of the chronicles of my friend, Mr Sherlock Holmes, cannot fail to have wondered what the high crimes and misdemeanours of the Professor were.

The reason why Holmes bestowed the appellation of the Napoleon of crime on Moriarty is set out below, and once readers have read the matters described, they will understand both why Holmes regarded Moriarty in the way that he did, and why this work's publication has been held back until long after the dead hand of time has taken its inevitable toll on all this drama's players.

I have related in my work, *The Empty House*, the events of April 1894, which resulted in the capture of Professor Moriarty's deputy, Colonel Moran, and the completely unanticipated return of my friend, Mr Sherlock Holmes, whom I had thought dead. I confess that even though my joy at his return was unconfined, I did wonder at the gullibility of Colonel Moran in being deceived by the silhouette of a wax bust of Holmes's head even if that silhouette were moved periodically by the redoubtable Mrs Hudson. I also wondered at Holmes's judgment in asking our aged landlady to change the bust's position when his plan was for the waxwork to be the target of a bullet fired by the finest shot in Europe. I had previously described Sherlock Holmes as the best and wisest man I had ever known, but, for all that his plan to capture Colonel Moran had succeeded beyond peradventure, it struck me then and strikes me now as highly questionable. But these reservations were set to one side on that glorious evening in 1894 as my friend, in form as good as I had ever seen him, sat once more in his familiar chair in our Baker Street sitting-room pointing out the infamy which attached to the letter M.

"Moriarty himself," he breezed exuberantly, pointing down at the voluminous file on his knee, "is enough to make any letter illustrious, and then there is Morgan the poisoner, Merridew of abominable memory, and Mathews, who knocked out my left canine in the waiting-room at Charing Cross. And, finally, here is our friend of tonight, Colonel Moran. I had previously appended a note that the Colonel was the second most dangerous man in London. Now," and the eyes of my friend shone with pride as he said this, "the deputy of the deceased Professor Moriarty will no longer be a factor in any future investigation."

Holmes paused and puffed on the cigar he had lit on our arrival at Baker Street. As the cigar's tip broke into a scarlet glow, I was captured by his mood and added.

"And don't forget Charles Augustus Milverton! Another M, the king of all the blackmailers and the worst man in London. That was how you described him at the time."

I was somewhat taken aback when this comment was greeted by a stony silence and Holmes stared into the distance. In an attempt to recapture the atmosphere that had obtained before I had mentioned Milverton, I asked a question that I had wanted clarity on ever since our precipitate flight to the Continent three years previously.

"So tell me, Holmes, what specific crimes Professor Moriarty was guilty of? Your brilliant capture of Colonel Moran tonight must have closed the whole matter off and so you can disclose them at last."

But, rather than removing the sudden careworn look on Holmes's face, this remark, even with the carefully selected and perhaps slightly dubious appellation of the word "brilliant," had the effect of making him look even more uncertain of himself. The puff on his cigar now seemed reflective rather than triumphant and it was not until he had drawn somewhat tentatively on it for a second time that he was able to respond.

"I fear, good Watson, that until Colonel Moran's trial has been completed, the crimes of the Professor himself will have to remain a secret even from you, who are my only friend, and who have faithfully reported only the things that I have sanctioned for disclosure to the general public. I cannot allow any risk of prejudicing the legal process and so the matter must remain *sub judice* while that process takes its course."

This latest response of Holmes puzzled me.

At my friend's specific request, the only charge to be brought against Colonel Moran was that of the murder in that same year of 1894 of Ronald Adair, who had accused Moran of cheating at cards. Hence Moran's trial would have nothing to do with anything the Colonel might ever have done in association with Moriarty who had met his end three years earlier, or indeed with either of Moran's two thwarted attempts on my friend's life. On the night of his capture, Moran had been in possession of the same unique air-rifle using the same soft bullets designed for a revolver that had been used to kill Ronald Adair. These bullets, as my friend put it, were, "enough to put Moran's head in a noose." I could see no difficulty in obtaining the necessary guilty verdict, but my certainty on this point was to prove to be unfounded.

The trial was held in June of the same year, and at it Moran's defence council entered a plea of insanity.

The prosecution, for its part, submitted that Moran's killing of Adair had been carefully planned and that he had used a ferocious weapon which could fire modified bullets in silence. "No crime," the prosecuting barrister stated in his concluding remarks to the jury, "could have been more meticulously planned or more ruthlessly carried out."

In his summing up to the jury, the judge drew the jurors' attention to Moran's long and honourable public service. "Colonel Moran," he said, "has served his country in the Jowaki Campaign and in the Afghan Campaign. He was mentioned in despatches for his work in Charasiab and he also distinguished himself in Sherpur and Kabul. In India he had crawled down a drain after a wounded man-eating tiger. Gentlemen of the jury, I would ask you to think long and hard before you return a simple guilty verdict even though on the facts, there can be no doubts as to who the killer of Ronald Adair was."

When the jurors came back into court, it was to deliver a verdict of guilty but insane and the judge ordered

4

that Moran be detained in a secure establishment until it was safe to release him.

My friend accepted the result with an unsurprised shrug and the most shocked reaction came from Lestrade who had played no more than a minor role in Moran's capture but who had made sure, to be fair with the consent of Holmes, that it was his own role in the arrest which had been trumpeted by the press. "I cannot believe the judge's summing up," fulminated Lestrade on one of his regular visits to Baker Street to seek my friend's advice. "If anyone acted with cunning and malice aforethought, it was Colonel Moran when he killed Adair. And yet now Moran will be held in agreeable conditions in some asylum until they find some doctor silly enough – apologies for impugning your profession, Dr Watson, but I have seen this all too often before – to declare him sane. And then he will be back out again and, you can sure, up to no good. Sentencing had got tougher during your absence, Mr Holmes, and the way judges summed up cases led to more guilty verdicts so as a result there were fewer felons engaged in their employment. A verdict and sentence like this one will only encourage more criminality."

Lestrade paused and lit a cigarette before he continued. "And having my prisoner sent to a secure establishment rather than to the gallows won't do much for my progression at Scotland Yard either."

My friend, who as the world's only consulting detective had no ambition of personal advancement, merely repeated his silent shrug while Lestrade vented his anger. As always, Holmes used his work as a way of blocking out anything else that might be troubling him and within a few months the two of us had been pitched into the complex cases of the papers of ex-President Murillo, and of the shocking affair of the Dutch steamship Friesland, which so nearly cost us both our lives. Before the matters I am about to discuss, the only occasion he referred to Moriarty at all was at the time of *The Norwood Builder* of 1894, amongst the very first cases he handled after his return, where he commented on Moriarty's masterminding of, "petty thefts, wanton assaults, purposeless outrage." At the time Holmes said this, I felt tempted to ask him if there were not some higher crimes that might have stemmed from the dread hand of Moriarty, but the dramatic entry into our quarters of the unhappy Mr John Hector McFarlane, the suspect in the apparent killing of the eponymous builder, drove the thought of doing so from my mind.

It was in one evening in early February 1899 that we received a visit from a man whose name I had mentioned at the time of *The Sign of Four* eleven years previously.

At the time of those events François Le Villard had come to the fore in the French detective service. He had consulted with Holmes and subsequently written him a letter containing a profusion of admiring comments with stray "magnifiques," "coups-de-maître," and "tours-de-force," all testifying to his regard for my friend. Now the card that preceded his arrival in our sitting-room declared Le Villard to be the head of the Paris police.

After Holmes had bestowed on the tall slim Frenchman rather more pleasantries than he was wont to bestow on Lestrade or any of his Scotland Yard colleagues, Le Villard came to the point.

"Paris is awash with rumours of an assassination plot against our Président, Félix Faure. Our last président but one, Président Carnot, was assassinated five years ago and so we are forced to take such rumours very seriously. Unfortunately, despite the warnings we have received, our président does not take his security seriously, and insists on continuing with the same routines as ever."

"An assassination plot in France!" exclaimed Holmes. "How very gr...disturbing."

"We are not sure who is behind this one – and you will *sans doute* form your own ideas, Mr Holmes – but we would like you to come to France to help us prevent any attempt from happening either by capturing the man behind the plot or by helping us to protect our président."

"I was just complaining to Dr Watson here about the singular lack of invention in the British criminal classes. An invitation to investigate the handiwork of their French counterparts is hard to resist. Good doctor," he said, turning to me, "pray bring your pistol on our forthcoming Parisian adventure and do not neglect to add to your luggage the very excellent field-glasses which you brought to the *Silver Blaze* case but never had the opportunity to use."

So it was that the following evening found us in Paris where Holmes and I had quarters in the comfortable Hôtel du Bois. On information as general as Le Villard had provided, my colleague's *modus operandi* was to consult widely with Le Villard's colleagues on the plausibility of the plot and to consult with the président's officials to try to get an understanding of the président's whereabouts and routines to devise ways to improve his protection. "This will all be brainwork rather than action, dear Watson, but you may, of course, join me if you wish," was how my colleague put it to me each morning and over the next three days, I learnt much about the président. I also learned about the anarchists who had been responsible for the assassination of the late Président Carnot – the assassin himself had been offered a chance to escape the guillotine if he disclosed who his fellow plotters were but had declined it – as well as about Communards, and disaffected members of the military.

On the fourth morning, Le Villard joined us at our breakfast table. After setting out an itinerary for the day ahead, he said to me, "Doctor Watson, I have arranged an appointment with the président's personal secretary, Monsieur Dupont, and he has insisted that only Mr Holmes and I should attend as he has some very – ahem – intimate matters to impart."

I felt nothing of substance had happened over the previous three days, and I was pleased to take some time out to see the sights of Paris. One obvious attraction was the Louvre and, as I was heading towards it from the hotel following the route prescribed by my tourist map, I passed along a minor thoroughfare called rue Chabanais.

My thoughts were all focused on the artistic delights that awaited me at the art-gallery but who was that knocking on the dark blue door of number 12 of that street?

Even having seen him only once in near darkness five years previously, I had given as full a description of him as I had of anyone whom I had encountered during my work with Holmes. Colonel Moran, I wrote at the time, had a tremendously virile and yet sinister face, the brow of a philosopher above and the jaw of a sensualist below allied with cruel blue eyes, a fierce, aggressive nose, and a threatening, deep-lined brow. Thus, I knew I could not be mistaken in identifying the sixty-year-old-man I could see in profile no more than a cricket-pitch's length from me as Colonel Moran, for all that he was meant to be incarcerated at Her Majesty's pleasure.

Before I could do anything more, I saw the door of number 12 open to admit him.

Was I, I asked myself, for once during the many years of my association with him, one step ahead of Sherlock Holmes? Was the man I saw before me the man who was plotting to kill the French président? Indeed, for what other reason might Colonel Moran be in Paris? And what was behind the anonymous looking door of 12 rue Chabanais?

I decided to seek entry myself and knocked on the door which opened at once.

It was a surprise when I entered from the February-coloured street, that, once admitted through the door of number 12, I was asked to wait in a small but beautifully appointed reception room. Costly tapestries covered the walls, fresh flowers – their brightness a miracle in this colourless season and emitting a bewitching fragrance in a crystal vase – stood on a marble topped table alongside a bowl of exotic and succulent fruit. I was soon joined by a tall, handsome, and formally dressed woman who looked stately now but who must have been of the utmost beauty a few years previously.

"Je m'appelle Madame Alexandrine Joannet," she said. "Comment puis-je vous aider?"

French is the language of love and even as my interlocutor said these few plain words, the heady scent of seduction was in the air.

"Parlez-vous anglais?" was all I could stutter in response, and I could feel my face reddening as I said it.

"I speak many tongues," replied she switching to English spoken in a rich Irish accent, and her smiling deep brown eyes looking searchingly into mine. "You look troubled, good sir. Perhaps you can say what is it you are seeking here?"

I was slightly unsure of what to say but in the end I confined myself to stammering, "I came here after a man. I had not anticipated that I would encounter a woman."

A look as of understanding came across the lady's face.

"I can assure you, sir, that once you cross our threshold all things are available freely at a price which will be outweighed manyfold by the unalloyed pleasure you will experience in finding what your heart desires."

The entrance to the premises I now found myself in had given me no clue as to what it was, but I was in no doubt now of what sort of establishment it was. I was wondering whether and how I should prolong the conversation when I heard an altercation coming from the inner courtyard.

"You cannot enter and then go *sans payer* – without paying – no matter how short your time here," an angry female voice said in heavily accented English – Japanese or Chinese, I fancied – although my exposure to the English of the far-east was limited.

"I got what I came in here for and, for what I sought, there can be no charge," came the angry reply in the Colonel's gruff voice which was unchanged from our brief encounter of five years previously.

I turned to the woman before me and said, "I fear there has been some misunderstanding on my part. I will leave immediately."

"God bless you, sir," replied she in her honeyed tone. "You are not the first to enter here under a misapprehension. But, as you will have heard, not everyone is so polite about such a misapprehension as you are. You may leave if you wish, and you may always return if your mind changes. Many of those who come in here under a misapprehension return once more. And sometimes many times more."

As I emerged back into the dull February light of rue Chabanais, I considered my options.

I did not know how long Moran's altercation might continue let alone what its outcome might be, and I doubted my ability to trail him undetected through Paris once he emerged. On the other hand, the presence in this city of someone who had twice tried to assassinate Holmes was something which my friend needed to be informed of, and I made my way to the Hotel du Bois as fast as I could.

"Colonel Moran has escaped," were the words with which my friend greeted me as I stepped into our quarters. "Because of the way security is run at Colney Hatch, it is not even clear when his escape was made. I have just received a verbose and querulous telegram from Lestrade about it."

"And I know where Colonel Moran is, for I have just seen him here in Paris," replied I, pleased for once truly to be in possession of better information than my friend and I explained what had happened at rue Chabanais.

"So, Moran has come here!" countered Holmes, sounding not at all surprised. "That is capital news! The plan I was formulating when I heard of his escape is dovetailing beautifully with our present investigation of the plot against the French president. After so many years of stagnation, at last we have a foeman worthy of my steel and a case that merits my intellect."

He paused and then lit a cigar in what I felt was a slightly premature act of triumph, before he continued talking out loud, but I had the sense that his words were addressed to himself rather than to me.

"So, Colonel Moran must have made his way straight to the establishment Dr Watson describes. That clears the most significant obstacle we face. I shall be very surprised if we cannot run him to ground here. I said of Professor Moriarty that I would regard my own destruction as a price worth paying for his, and I would say the same in the case of Moran. And events have conspired that we may have come here to Paris just in time to prevent an imperial crisis."

"You would lay down your life to prevent a crisis in the French Empire?" I asked interrupting his soliloquy. Holmes had never shown any sign of interest in the well-being of France and so his concerns about an imperial crisis came as a surprise to me. "And have you no concerns as to your own safety even though you are in the same city as a man so dangerous he tried to kill twice?"

My friend stared straight ahead once more, and, as ever, I knew better than to press either line of questioning.

Instead, I asked another question. "What are we going to do?"

"I am going to smoke, and the final details will occur to me."

My friend now switched to cigarettes, but, contrary to his normally lengthy deliberations, he was no more than halfway through his second cigarette when he drew himself up and again spoke as if to himself rather than addressing me.

"The Colonel is fresh arrived in Paris. He will have been commissioned to come here and will have been briefed. It must be overwhelmingly likely that he will strike tonight for if he does not he will soon make Paris too hot to hold him. My very simple stratagem of laying a baited trap to deceive the old *shakiri* succeeded once before. Why should it not do so again now?" Then turning to me, he said. "I will be reconnoitring this afternoon, but I would not undertake so bold an adventure as I plan this evening without my Boswell at my side. I would beg you not to leave our quarters here while I am absent."

Holmes strode out of the door without another word leaving me at something of a loose end, but he was back by half-past-four.

"Come, good Watson. We have an assignation outside the Elysée Palace in rue du Faubourg Saint-Honoré. Please bring the service pistol and the field-glasses. And when we take up our station, no sound louder than a whisper."

It was already dark by the time we reached the rue du Faubourg Saint-Honoré, "So much the better," whispered Holmes as we positioned ourselves in the deep shadow of a doorway.

The street was lit and on the other side of the road – no more than fifty paces from us – we could see the palace. The ground floor was in darkness, but the rooms of its upper floor were brilliantly lit. Just as I had been able to see the bust of Holmes moving in the Baker Street sitting-room from our position in the empty house opposite 221 B in 1894, so it was that now I could see undefined movement in one of these first-floor windows. I put my glasses to my eye to see in more detail, and saw to my astonishment, the outline of a couple writhing at the level of the window. I was about to whisper to Holmes what I could see when as if out of nowhere a dark figure with a gun at his shoulder took up a position immediately before us. But before the gunman could set himself, Holmes leapt forward onto his back, and I followed an instant afterwards just in time to hear the hiss of an air-rifle discharge a bullet which whizzed past my shoulder. But, as five years previously, in this battle with the would-be assassin, Holmes and I had the advantage of numbers and of surprise, and within a few seconds the noise of the altercation brought the footsteps of the gendarmerie running.

Soon in the pale street lamplight we could see the face of Colonel Moran as he was held by three French officers.

If the Colonel's reaction to his capture five years earlier had been ungracious, his fury at this second apprehension was even greater. This fury increased as Holmes searched his pockets and his arm had to be twisted right behind his back by the gendarmes as Holmes drew out a sealed envelope which was concealed inside the Colonel's jacket. "And that, I fancy, will be that," said my friend with an air of satisfaction as he held it up in the light of the gas-lamps.

In a show of superhuman strength, Moran briefly escaped the grasp of the French officers and lunged at the envelope as my friend continued to hold it aloft, but the officers were able to recover control and cuff him.

We were joined by Le Villard.

"Let us go the Palace," said he. "I had extra panes of glass installed in the window where the Président normally entertains his mistress every Thursday evening so the couple you had installed there were in no danger."

As we arrived at the Palace a functionary dashed up to us. "Les médecins déjà! Vous étès arrivés vite! Je pense que le Président est encore en vie."

"What do you mean the président is still alive," said Holmes looking mortified. "And why have you sent for doctors? I gave clear instructions that the président should entertain his mistress in a different room this evening so that he would be in no danger."

"Don't forget, Holmes, Moran was able to discharge one bullet before we took him into custody," I pointed out to Holmes although from my friend's ashen expression, I could see he needed no reminding of this.

We were joined by Faure's personal secretary, M Dupont, whom Holmes and Le Villard had had an appointment with that morning.

"I am a doctor," I said to Dupont, "although I am here by chance. If a doctor is needed, let me see your président whatever room he is in."

We were taken into a reception room in which a man of sixty, I assumed Président Faure, was lying, his modesty protected only by a flimsy white gown. He was still breathing but beyond speech and it was obvious his demise was at most minutes away.

"This is the greatest blow of my career," said Holmes over and over again.

I performed a quick examination.

"There is no wound on him."

"Hélas, in spite of the danger we told him he was in," said Dupont, "Monsieur le Président insisted on seeing his *maîtresse* this evening as he does every Thursday evening. His preference is to, *ahem*, enjoy her embrace on the presidential desk in the Salon d'argent or silver reception-room at the front of the building but because of your very explicit warnings about an assassination attempt, Mr Holmes, he and his partner took up residence in a room at the back of the building."

"I am relieved to hear it," said my friend.

"I fear that Monsieur le Président struggles with the fourth line of the *Marseillaise?*"

"He struggles with the fourth line of the *Marseillaise?*" asked my friend, a look of unwonted bafflement coming over his face.

"Yes, the line is about raising a standard aloft, and I fear that our aged Président cannot raise his own standard aloft without taking a special preparation of quinine. He took a double dose this evening and that caused a seizure in him as he lay in the embrace of his mistress, Madame Marguerite Steinheil."

"His habits sound like those of our own Prince of Wales," I murmured, shocked by the turn of events.

"As the seizure took hold of Monsieur Faure," continued Dupont, "Madame Steinheil broke out into screams. As the président's private secretary, I have a free hand to enter his quarters as I see the need and, when I heard the screams, I broke into here. I found the président's hand caught up irretrievably in the lady's hair and I had to

17

apply a pair of scissors to her locks to disentangle her from him."

"Where is Madame Steinheil now?"

"She was allowed to dress, and her departure from the scene has been facilitated through the rear exit of the Palace. I fear such goings on are not unusual with our presidents who have traditionally kept a string of mistresses at an age when – well, perhaps at an age when such a thing is unwise."

I had another look at the expiring politician.

"This looks a clear case of apoplexy. There is, as I have said, no wound, and the rictus on the patient's face is consistent with an internal trauma rather than being due to any external factor." As I said this, Monsieur Faure took a deep breath, opened his eyes briefly to look around him, and then took his leave of this life.

There seemed nothing more to say and Le Villard was anxious to update us on matters which Holmes obviously knew about but I did not.

"Your *collaboratrice* in this matter, Mr Holmes, your associate Madame Joannet, is of course known to us in the French police as the proprietress of Le Chabanais as it is one of the *maisons publiques* of Paris frequented by all of the city's top society and by many distinguished foreign visitors as well. She and her associate" – he paused to consider the right word – "disported themselves before the window in the way you requested and attracted the attention of your would-be assassin. The precaution you had suggested of fitting extra panes of glass to the window of the salon, meant that they were in no danger even if the assassin had succeeded in hitting the palace. So, I can assure you, our président's death had nothing do with your attempts to protect him, Mr Holmes," concluded Le Villiard, paying no heed to me.

It was not long before we were joined by Madame Joannet herself who entered the reception room as though she knew it well. She had a beautiful Oriental female companion with her.

"The act in the window you asked us to put on, Mr Holmes, was a matter of the greatest simplicity for someone like me," said she in her warm Irish voice to my companion. "I have had to put on performances like that for our clients many times before." She turned to glance at her associate. "I have always found it much easier to engage another a woman for such a task as women have a natural understanding for the idea that what we are doing is an act. Mee Wye here carried her role off to perfection."

"I can assure you, Madame Joannet, it is always a joy to be of service to you," said Madame Joannet's companion with an accent similar to that which I had heard that morning in the altercation with Colonel Moran but now melded with an exotic sweetness.

"You put yourselves in the greatest danger," said my friend, "and I am relieved that you came to no harm."

"Bless you, Mr Holmes. When I heard that you had had extra glass fitted in the window, I knew you had taken all the necessary precautions. In the line of work my associate and I do, rather like in yours, it is a question of exposing yourself to danger while taking every precaution against it. It would be a great pleasure if you and the Doctor were to visit our establishment tomorrow. Our clientele consists mostly of those who owe their status to their birth and not to making their own way in the world as you and I have done. Thus, a visit from you and Dr Watson would be an honour indeed for le Chabanais."

"I fear we will be fully occupied with sorting out the consequences of what has happened here tonight," replied Holmes to Madame Joannet's proposition, a ghost of a smile flitting across his face.

"As you wish Mr Holmes. We will be open for business as usual, should either you or Dr Watson change your mind. And, of course, we would be honoured to welcome you and your friend either together or singly at any other time in the future."

And with that Madame Joannet walked out of the Elysée Palace with her beautiful companion beside her.

"Her real name is Madame Kelly, and she is originally from Dublin though she speaks French without an accent," Le Villiard told us looking as though star-struck at the back of the departing madame. "I have also heard her speak Spanish, Italian, German, and Flemish in her line of work."

"How will the death of the président be presented to the public?"

"We will confine our announcement to saying he died of apoplexy and the fact that that is the diagnosis of perhaps the best known *médecin* in the world, Dr Watson," – the

Frenchman turned to bow to me at this point, – "will mean that no one will query it. Apoplexy can cover a multitude of sins. As I recall, Mr Holmes, apoplexy was the cause of death ascribed to Colonel Barclay in *The Crooked Man*, although the background to his death was a good deal more complicated than what that eight-letter word suggests."

"And what will happen to Colonel Moran?"

"I am sure you will understand in circumstances such as these, we will want to keep possible scrutiny of the published facts to the minimum. Thus, we will not want to bring charges against Colonel Moran of attempted assassination to court. But I am also sure that if the British authorities ask for the extradition of a person who has previously committed murder while insane, their French counterparts will look with favour on the request as they will want to be rid of someone who is an unwelcome guest in our country."

There seemed nothing more to be said and Holmes and I returned to our hotel. There was still time for us to catch the night express to Calais and we were back in Baker Street by lunchtime the following day.

My friend was in a thoughtful mood.

"So we have prevented the assassination of the président who has died in circumstance the details of which cannot be disclosed to the public. And we have prevented a scandal that would have rocked the Empire."

I felt I might learn more from my friend if I said nothing, so I merely drew at my pipe.

My approach proved the right one as my friend continued.

"The beryl coronet is one of the most precious possessions of the Empire as you described in your work of that name."

Again, I drew at my pipe and said nothing.

At length, Holmes rose from his seat and went to his files.

"And this photograph is at the heart of one of the greatest secrets of the Empire."

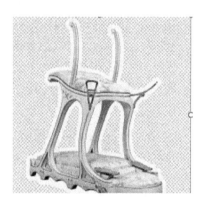

I looked down at the photograph he had placed on the little table before me and reproduce it to the left of this page.

I stared at it for some time before I asked in some wonderment, "What is it?" I asked at last.

"The Prince of Wales is a habitue of the establishment you visited, Le Chabanais. He has recourse to it when he seeks his pleasure there. The prince's other vice is gluttony. He routinely eats a twelve-course dinner, and his consequent great girth means his amorous activities are hamstrung by the danger of him crushing his partner underneath him. This device means he can stand to take his pleasure and the lower cushions, I understand, are for a second partner to lie and provide additional intimacies."

"But there is nothing to connect the Prince of Wales with this," – I struggled for a word and then opted for – "piece of furniture." And, indeed, there is nothing to indicate when or where this photograph was taken, and based on what I can see in the picture no can say for certain what this seat's use was, for all that you have provided an explanation."

"It is called *Le siège de la volupté* – the seat of pleasure,"

"Good heavens! And what has this to do with the matter we have been investigating?"

"You will recall my reluctance to confirm my previous accolade of the master of blackmail on Charles Augustus Milverton on the night we captured Colonel Moran. It is because Professor Moriarty was using this chair to blackmail the British Government."

"How could the Professor blackmail the British government using this when there is nothing visible to connect the Prince with it and so any association is easily denied?"

"Moriarty had a photograph of the Prince of Wales *in flagrante* as he made use of this chair and he threatened to publish it. But no one knew where Moriarty kept it. I found this photograph of the chair *sans* the prince, when, at the request of the British government, I went through the documents kept in Professor Moriarty's study. If the photograph of the Prince disporting himself in this chair had become known to the general public, this country and its great Empire would become the subject of ridicule, and who knows where the contagion might stop." My reader may recall that I was not even allowed to disclose that my friend had been in Moriarty's office until I published *The Valley of Fear* in 1914 although the events described in that work occurred in the 1880s.

"So what form did the blackmail take?" I asked.

"It is hard to blackmail a jury because a jury's members are randomly selected. But when a particularly notorious criminal was up for sentencing, Moriarty would demand a low sentence as his price for not leaking this photograph of the Prince of Wales making use of this chair and the government would apply pressure on the judge in the case to pass a low sentence. Moriarty would then collect a fee from the prisoner. When word of this got around, criminals would approach Moriarty before they undertook a job and pay him a commission to ensure they got a lower sentence if caught. Lestrade noticed this and commented that the length of sentences handed down had increased when I was assumed to have died. I expect that sentences will increase again now."

"So he turned the criminality of others into his own business?"

"That was his *modus operandi*. It was in the hope of retrieving it from Moriarty that made me choose a place where I might wrestle with him in the hope of retrieving the photograph from him in the struggle. But alas, it was to no avail. That photograph had made Moriarty exceedingly wealthy and I feel his success with it meant that he usurped even the claim of Charles Augustus Milverton as the master of blackmail."

"So what happened when Moriarty died?"

"After I had failed to find it on Moriarty's person, I always suspected that the Professor must have told Moran its whereabouts. That suspicion was confirmed when the judge directed the jury in the way that he did at Moran's trial. My difficulty in preventing its future use once Moran escaped from the asylum lay in that I did not know where the photograph was. But your chance sighting of Moran and the conversation you reported he had had with the courtesan suggested to me that he had concealed the photograph at Le Chabanais, and that when you saw him, he had gone there to retrieve it. I could not believe he would let it off his person and you saw his furious reaction when I abstracted it from him as his hold on the British government was now forever broken."

"And what will you do with it now?"

"I have always sought to be more than a mere criminal investigator, good Watson," said my friend. "I see my role more as someone who dispenses justice. I act as investigator, jury, and judge. In this latter role I take my own decisions about thieves and killers on whether to let normal justice to take its course or to set them free. In taking those decisions I might be seen by some as having committed crimes myself. I suspect having in my strongbox this photograph," – he held up the still sealed envelope – "of the Prince of Wales making vigorous use of *Le siège de la volupté* will protect me from any pressure which may be applied by the British government. I will thus be able me to turn the use of this photograph from the evil it has served in the past to good in the future."

"If you wish," I offered, "I can add this photograph to the documents I deposit for posterity at Cox & Co, my bankers. It will always retrievable and yet no document I have ever placed there has returned into public circulation."

Holmes sat in thought for a while and then took the envelope from his strongbox.

"Let us to your bank now and place this envelope there now before it closes."

I think he was flattered when I said to him, "You are truly humanity's benefactor," as we headed down the stairs.

"It is I," said she, "the woman whose life you have ruined."

Milverton laughed, but fear vibrated in his voice. "You were so very obstinate," he said. "Why did you drive me to such extremities? I assure you I wouldn't hurt a fly of my own accord, but every man has his business, and what was I to do? I put the price well within your means. You would not pay."

"So you sent the letters to my husband, and he—the noblest gentleman that ever lived, a man whose boots I was never worthy to lace—he broke his gallant heart and died. You never thought to see me here again, but it was that night which taught me how I could meet you face to face, and alone."

The woman stood with her hand buried in her bosom, and a deadly smile played on her thin lips.

"You will ruin no more lives as you have ruined mine. You will wring no more hearts as you have wrung mine. I will free the world of a poisonous thing. Take that, you hound—and that!—and that!—and that!"

She drew a little gleaming revolver, and emptied barrel after barrel into

Milverton's body, the muzzle within two feet of his shirt front. He fell forward upon the table, coughing furiously and clawing among the papers, received another shot, and rolled upon the floor. "You've done me," he cried, and lay still. The woman looked down at him intently, and then ground her heel into his upturned face. The curtains rustled as they parted, the night air blew into the heated room, and the avenger was gone.

As I remarked when I published my account of events, the death of the master of blackmail, Charles Augustus Milverton, at the hands of one of his blackmail victims was quite unique among those adventures of my friend that I elected to set before the public, and the above quotes directly from it. Holmes and I had gone to Milverton's Hampstead house, Appledore Towers, with the intent of breaking his safe and destroying the material he used for blackmailing within it. The completely unanticipated killing the two of us witnessed from behind a curtain in Milverton's study was the only killing that happened before my eyes, the only case involving a female killer, and the only matter that my friend declined to pursue when invited to do so.

I suspect that it was because of the grotesqueness of the killing, another matter which I mentioned in my account of events has attracted much less attention from followers of my friend's activities than one might otherwise have expected. To spy on Milverton, Holmes had disguised himself as a rakish young workman, with a goatee beard, a swagger, and a clay-pipe. I set out below the extraordinary exchange that arose between us when Holmes was taking a break from his investigation and was back at Baker Street.

"You would not call me a marrying man, Watson?"

"No, indeed!"

"You'll be interested to hear that I am engaged."

"My dear fellow! I congrat—"

"To Milverton's housemaid."

"Good heavens, Holmes!"

"I wanted information, Watson."

"Surely you have gone too far?"

"It was a most necessary step. I am a plumber with a rising business, Escott, by name. I have walked out with Agatha each evening, and I have talked with her. Good heavens, those talks! However, I have got all I wanted. I know Milverton's house as I know the palm of my hand."

"But the girl, Holmes?"

My friend shrugged his shoulders.

"You can't help it, my dear Watson. You must play your cards as best you can when such a stake is on the table. However, I rejoice to say that I have a hated rival, who will certainly cut me out the instant that my back is turned."

The morning after the killing of Milverton, as Holmes and I sat over our morning pipes, Inspector Lestrade came to Baker Street to ask us to investigate the case.

I had all but been caught by Milverton's under-gardener as I scrambled over a wall to flee the scene of the crime and the under-gardener had given Lestrade a description of one of the two men whom he had nearly caught and who, inevitably, were believed to be the prime suspects in Milverton's killing. It was no surprise that the description – strongly built, moustache, square jaw – bore a striking similarity to me. Holmes and Lestrade made merry over this similarity. I affected to share this merriment, but I felt a sense of foreboding that this would not be the last we heard of the matter.

As we sat at lunch that day, Holmes had sprung from his seat, and we had dashed in a hansom to Regent Circus where, in a shop-window filled with photographs of the celebrities and beauties of the day, he had shown me a picture of the noble lady who had carried out the killing that he and I had been witness to. Holmes put his forefinger to his lips so that I would say nothing and when I published my account of events in 1904, I declined to name the killer, the year, or even the decade in which the events had occurred.

On the late afternoon of the day after the killing, Holmes stood at the window and looked down at the street below while I sat engrossed in a medical paper. Suddenly I heard my friend utter an inarticulate cry, panic-stricken in a way I had never heard from him previously.

"Great Scott!" he exclaimed, and darted out of the sitting room and across the corridor into his own bedroom into which I had never until then ventured in all my years of sharing quarters with him. I followed to see him throw up the sash-window and leap from it into the upper branches of one of the trees in the courtyard behind the building which housed our flat. "Close the window and the door of the room behind me!" he cried to me as he leapt. The last I saw of him was his dark shadow as he disappeared into the deepening twilight over the roof of the building behind.

I did as bidden and returned to the sitting room. But before I had a chance to sit down, and with the cold blast of air from opening the window of Holmes's bedroom still palpable in the sitting-room, the buttons announced, "Miss Agatha Brown!"

A tall, dark-haired woman in her early twenties entered, and said as she came through the door, "I am here to see Mr Sherlock Holmes."

"I am afraid he is not here at present," I replied with as much composure as I could muster. "And I fear," and here I clutched gratefully at having something I could say with utter truthfulness as I tried not to let my alarm show at what I could see was coming next, "I do not know when he will be back."

Miss Brown, a woman of obviously simple means, dissolved into tears.

"Is there no one who will help me find Mr Escott?" she wailed. "Mr Holmes is my only hope."

"Mr Escott?" asked I, trying to sound as though I had never before heard the name.

"Are you Mr Holmes's colleague, Dr Watson?" asked she.

I confined myself to a stiff nod.

"I am the housemaid of Mr Charles Augustus Milverton at Appledore Tower in Hampstead. I had been being courted by Mr Caldwell, the under-gardener. But we had had a falling out, and Mr Escott came into my life, and swept me off my feet. And then last night, Mr Milverton was shot dead. The police have been all over the place. I am sure they will ask whether any strangers have been hanging round Appledore Towers. I don't know what to do."

She paused before imparting her dilemma though I could sense what was going to say.

"Do I tell Inspector Lestrade – that's the name of the policeman in charge – about Mr Escott?" she eventually came out with. "My fiancé appeared as if from nowhere and I've been walking out with him for two weeks. But he didn't come round on the night of the killing nor the night before last nor last night. He was with me at every hour that I was off shift before then. I don't know what has become of him. And that's why I've come to see Mr Holmes."

She looked up at me with desperate eyes.

"If I tell Mr Lestrade that I have a fiancé who has disappeared, the inspector may find my Mr Escott, but it may be that I will have given him away as a murderer, and he could be for the rope."

My reader may imagine my horror at the turn of events.

If Miss Brown were able to give Lestrade a description of Mr Escott which bore any similarity to my friend, surely even Lestrade could hardly fail to notice the coincidence of two men one of whom bore a resemblance to Holmes and the other to me being at Appledore Towers at the time Milverton was killed.

Miss Brown broke down once more into sobs and, as I waited for her to regain her composure, I considered my options.

I could decline to help her in any way but that could only make her more likely to tell Lestrade about her association with the vanished Mr Escott and who knows what she might reveal and what Lestrade might make of it? Or I could confide to Miss Brown that her Mr Escott had been my friend in disguise. But I could quite imagine the effect that such a disclosure would have on her feelings quite apart from the very real danger that that would make her even more likely to denounce my friend and me to Lestrade. Or I could play for time in the hope that my friend could resolve matters when – the conjunction "when" seemed something of a flight of optimism in this instance – he returned.

"Would you be able to help me, Dr Watson, if Mr Holmes is not around?" came the question from Miss Brown to interrupt my musings and in the end I felt I had no option but to try to engage with her.

"What can you tell me about Mr Escott?" I asked, in what even I realised was a forlorn hope that there might be another Mr Escott apart from the jobbing plumber Holmes had invented.

"He's a jobbing plumber. He told me about how he's been getting all manner of jobs around Hampstead. Doing very well for himself, he was. But now he's upped and gone."

"Can you give me a description of Mr Escott?"

"Very nicely spoken. And tall and slim. And he smoked a clay pipe. I like that in a man."

"Anything else?" I asked, relieved beyond measure that Miss Brown's description of my friend was so vague as not to identify him.

Miss Brown paused.

"And his top corner tooth on his left side was missing."

I felt an instant chill.

This was a detail I had relayed to my readers about my friend in *The Empty House.*

The felon Matthews, in one of the matters I have still to put to paper, had given my friend a right-hook which had

33

knocked out Holmes's left canine in the waiting-room at Charing Cross Station as my friend arrested him. If, I mused, Miss Brown could give a description containing this detail, it was hard to see even Lestrade not noting the similarity of Miss Brown's Mr Escott to my friend.

"You must give me some time to think," I said in the end trying to keep a note of desperation out of my voice. "Where can I contact you?"

"I'm still living at the Towers though I don't know what will happen now that Mr Milverton is no more. Such a kind master he was to his servants. Now I've got no fiancé, and no home. I don't know what will become of me," and with that despairing remark Miss Brown withdrew leaving me to contemplate a case to which I knew the true solution, but had the strongest reasons for finding an alternative and false one, and no Sherlock Holmes to help me do so.

I was still sat wondering what to do next when the buttons appeared once more at the door this time to announce the return of Inspector Lestrade.

"I was hoping Mr Holmes would be here," he said his face falling when I informed him of Holmes's absence for an undefined period. "We have had a striking development in the Appledore Towers case. I really think what I have found would appeal to Mr Holmes. He might even reconsider his decision not to take on this case."

He paused to light a cigar.

"You will recall, Dr Watson," went on Lestrade with the air of someone desperate to tell someone what he had on his chest much though I did not want to hear any more about the Milverton case, "that we had assumed that the two intruders who were chased by the gardening staff were responsible for the killing."

"Yes," I said uneasily.

"And you will recall we have a description of one the two intruders whom the under-gardener nearly caught. And we have also got footprints of both."

"So you said when you were here the day before yesterday," I replied with an even greater sense of unease and extending my legs so that my feet were beneath the low table that stood between the two armchairs before the hearth and making sure they were flat to the floor so that my soles of my shoes were completely invisible.

"When we examined the body of the deceased in detail," continued Lestrade, speaking as though he were addressing Holmes rather than me, "we found his face had been disfigured. It had marks on it consistent with someone grinding their heel into it as the victim lay dead. We examined the wound in detail and what do you think we found?"

I was trying to say as little as possible so as not to incriminate myself, so I confined myself to trying to look as though I were curious.

"The heel of the shoe had a pointed tip," continued Lestrade, warming to his theme. "What do you deduce from that?"

"That there was a third intruder, and that this third intruder was a woman?" I suggested, trying to make something that I already knew sound as if I had thought it out for myself.

"You've obviously been learning from Mr Holmes, Dr Watson," said Lestrade, sounding impressed, although looking slightly disappointed that he could not surprise me with this detail. "And this third intruder must have left separately from the two other intruders as no mention of a third person was made by the staff who gave the first two intruders chase."

I paused to think before saying, "This is doubtless very interesting, Inspector, to someone whose specialism is crime, but investigation of it is really a matter for Mr Holmes rather than for me if he chooses to become involved. I cannot tell you when he will be back, but I will pass on the information you have imparted."

I think Lestrade was again slightly disappointed, this time by my lack of excitement at what he was saying, though my outward calm concealed a pounding heart as the twin prospect of Holmes and me facing a capital trial and of the prospect of Milverton's true killer being discovered became closer. In the end Lestrade took himself off and I was left to profoundly uncomfortable thoughts.

And yet Lestrade was not the last visitor of the day for, as I lay sleepless in bed, there was a tap on the window. Holmes had climbed a drainpipe which ran down from the roof past my bedroom window. I lit a candle and raised the sash, the flame of the candle flickering alarmingly in the cold night air as I did so. When he spoke, Holmes talked in breathless gasps with the effort of holding onto the pipe.

"I won't come in," he hissed. "I am in one of my hide-aways. If you need to get hold of me, leave a message at the Wimpole Street Post Office. And keep Miss Brown engaged for the next few days. It will stop her talking to Lestrade."

"Lestrade knows that there was a woman at the scene. And Miss Brown says that her Mr Escott had his left upper canine tooth missing. Like you do."

"All the more reason to keep Miss Brown otherwise engaged and away from Lestrade."

"How do you propose I should do that?"

Holmes was hanging from a drainpipe so it was hard for him to shrug but there was a note of indifference in his voice as he said, "Well, she will be underoccupied as her master is dead and when she was occupied with her domestic duties, she always found time to see me."

"So you want me to tie her up with an investigation which you want me to conduct and to which I already know the solution?"

"Do you have an alternative plan?"

As it happened I had formulated one.

"What if I walked along a riverside with Miss Brown and pushed her into the water? As you in your disguise as Mr Escott as are so skilled at befriending domestic staff, you could be walking by the river with her former admirer, Mr Caldwell, the under-gardener. It could be he who dives into the water to rescue her and so he and she might be reconciled."

"Well," said Holmes, "that is certainly one possible approach," although his voice betrayed no enthusiasm for my idea.

"It is you, Holmes, I normally look to for a plan."

There was a long silence, and I was waiting for Holmes to say something definitive. In the end all he came out with was, "I will have to come back to you with one."

"When?" I asked.

"When one has occurred to me."

And with this troubling response my friend slid from view down the drainpipe.

The next day I sent a message to Miss Brown arranging to meet her at a café in Hampstead.

"I can get the time off easy at the moment," she said, as she arrived, "as there are no duties with Mr Milverton being no more. But I can't afford to come to a place like this."

"My friend and colleague Mr Holmes only charges to defray his costs except when he chooses to remit them altogether," I replied, myself slightly uneasy at being in a café in a suburb as fashionable as Hampstead when I was not so well-heeled myself. "Where used you to meet Mr Escott?" – and I found myself all but saying Mr Holmes.

A slight blush crossed Miss Brown's cheeks at the recollection of her beau.

"We used to walk across the heath. It's a popular spot for couples without much money if you see what I mean."

"And what did Mr Escott tell you about himself?"

"I never found out where he lived but he talked a lot about plumbing. Ball cocks were a speciality of his. Funnily enough, he said the secret of his success as a plumber was because for a first job he would often only look to cover his costs and would sometimes decide not to take any payment at all if he thought there might be repeat business. Your Mr Holmes sounds very like my Mr Escott from what you say."

She paused and stared at me, and I held my counsel for fear of saying something incriminating.

"Mr Escott was always very interested in what I do," she continued. "I think he was wondering if there might be a plumbing job for him at the Towers as he wanted to find out the layout of all the bathrooms. Or do you think he wanted to know the lay out to carry out a different kind of job?"

"I cannot yet speculate as to your fiancé's motives for wanting to know about the house," I said, trying as far as possible to give responses which did not result in me telling a direct lie to Miss Brown, "but I am sure there will have been one and you suggesting possibilities is the best way of finding the right one. And what else did he talk about?"

"He was very clever at noticing things about people. As we walked along, he would tell me about the people he saw. He could spot a left-handed man by his shave. He said a right-handed-man would always do a better job of shaving the left side of his face so if you saw stubble on a man's left cheek, he was probably left-handed. For a young girl like me, it was amazing to listen to him. In fact," she continued, "it was remembering tricks like that that made me think of Mr Sherlock Holmes when my Mr Escott disappeared."

Holmes as a wooer and as a consulting detective were not as different as I might have expected, I mused, and I very much feared that if Lestrade interviewed Miss Brown, even he might not have too many difficulties realising that a man who looked like Sherlock Holmes, thought like Sherlock Holmes, and had an associate who looked the same as an associate of Sherlock Holmes, probably was Sherlock Holmes. And that if the man who had nearly been caught fleeing from the scene of the murder of Charles Augustus Milverton looked like Dr John Watson and associated with a man who probably was Sherlock Holmes, then the other man probably was Dr John Watson.

"What is happening at the house?" I asked, hoping to direct the conversation into less dangerous waters.

"The police are still all over the place. They have done a finger-tip search of the building and all the outbuildings and are doing the same with the grounds. The word among the staff is that Mr Milverton was meeting an outside party with whom he had an appointment. Interviewing the domestic staff is not a priority, although they have given Mr Milverton's secretary, Mr Dawber, a long interview."

"So will they not interview you at all?"

"They have said they will see the domestics tomorrow."

"Tomorrow?" I started. "And what have you decided to tell them about Mr Escott?" I asked hoping against hope that Miss Brown would have resolved to say nothing about her association with my friend.

Tears again came into Miss Brown's eyes. "I do not know. I was hoping Mr Holmes might be able to help me with that if you cannot."

There seemed nothing more to say and I returned to Baker Street though not before I had left a note at the Wimpole Street Post Office to tell Holmes the outcome of my discussions with Miss Brown. That night I fell into a fitful sleep and woke with a start to find my room feeling suddenly cold. I lit a candle and realised that the sash had been raised from the outside (who else might have done that but Holmes?) and a note left saying, "Meet me at the entrance to Appledore Towers at noon."

I could not imagine why Holmes might want to take the risk of going there but let the matter pass.

Noon saw me, filled with dread, at Appledore Towers. Holmes was waiting at the entrance, dressed in his own smart but under-stated style, and looking anything but like a man who had been living in a hideaway and climbing drainpipes in the dark.

"It is all working out wonderfully well," said he. "Let us go the house where Lestrade is waiting for us. I would advise you, good Watson, that Lestrade is bound to ask you your opinion on a point in this case which requires your opinion as a man with a medical background."

"What do you want me to say?" I asked, dreading I might be asked to lie.

"You must respond with a precise description of exactly what you saw on the night of Milverton's death."

"Are you sure that that is wise, Holmes?" I asked.

"Pray respond saying exactly what you saw," was all my friend would say.

Lestrade was waiting for us on the porch of Appledore Towers, and we knocked on the door.

A butler opened the door.

"I have gathered all the domestic staff except Miss Brown in the drawing room, Inspector, as you requested."

"Thank you, Broderick," replied Lestrade. "There are just a couple of points I would like to clear with these gentlemen before I see the staff," he added nodding at Holmes and me. "Miss Brown is the housemaid," he added – as if Holmes and I needed any reminding, and her absence set my mind racing at what she might have said. "At her request, I saw her first thing this morning." Lestrade turned back to Broderick. "I asked that Mr Milverton's body be returned here by my men and placed back in his study in the position in which it was found."

"That has happened, Inspector. Your men were considerate enough to use the study's French windows to return the body, Inspector, rather than bringing it through the house and I welcome their consideration for the staff here who are much disturbed by the death of Mr Milverton."

Lestrade, Holmes, and I went into the study.

"The case seemed so easy," grunted the professional. "We nearly had our hands on two man of whom we had descriptions and then found that a woman had ground her pointed heel into the face of the victim. But here we have Milverton's body back and, as far as possible, placed exactly as we found it. And a surgeon has extracted the bullets from it. They are here in this vial," and, he held up a glass container with what I saw were five tiny bullets still smeared with blood. "I must admit that this all feels like going back to square one."

It was a strange feeling for me to see the study by daylight after the drama of my last visit.

"I take it you have conducted a thorough search of this room, Inspector?" asked Holmes.

"I have not done so myself, of course, but I am assured by my men that they have been over it with a fine-toothed comb," said Lestrade, "but..."

"Then perhaps you can explain why they missed the weapon that was used. See, it is there in the corner."

Holmes dived into a dark corner of the room and came up holding the little gleaming revolver I had seen a few brief nights previously. Lestrade stared.

"Perhaps you might show me the vial with the bullets again, Inspector. See," continued Holmes, pointing at the revolver's muzzle, "the small bore of the gun is consistent with the small size of the bullets although a microscopic examination will have to be conducted to conclude whether this was the weapon used to fire them."

"I will demand an explanation from Parker why he did not find this," exclaimed Lestrade, and stormed out of the room.

As soon as he was gone, Holmes stooped over a low metal-framed occasional table, but he had drawn himself up to his normal height by the time Lestrade had returned with his red-faced colleague.

"We were looking for prints not a weapon," said Parker defensively, "so we would hardly look into a corner of the room. With the resources we get, we need to make our searches where we are likeliest to find what we are looking for."

"If I may interject in Sergeant Parker's defence," said Holmes calmly, "I only formed my alternative view of this case after several days of contemplation. And even then I did not think I would find a weapon as quickly as I did until I looked at the dead man's body."

"What has the dead man's body got to do with where the weapon was found?"

"If you look at Milverton's face, his shave is much closer on the right side of his face which suggests that he was left-handed. When he shot himself, the pistol was going to fall from his hand to the left side of where his body lay so a corner to his left side was an obvious place to look for an undiscovered weapon. The handedness of the owner of a body is often of as much importance in a case as the handedness of a killer."

"So what is your theory of what has happened, Mr Holmes?" asked Lestrade, his eyes wide in wonder.

"Suicide."

"Suicide?" Lestrade looked astonished at my friend's theory. "But that goes against all the facts. Milverton's face had been disfigured by someone grinding a pointed heel into it. That could only be a woman who was a third person on the scene."

"Look at the corner of this table." Holmes stooped once more where he had stooped while Lestrade had been absent. "See, there is a bloodstain on it. This must be where Milverton struck himself as he fell. I only found it because I was looking for it. The theory that the disfigured face was caused by someone grinding their heel into it may have come from someone with an eye for theatre."

"Why did you not see the stain on this table, Parker?" demanded Lestrade, I think not really listening to what my friend had said.

"We were looking for footprints, Inspector. We would not look for such prints on the corner of a table. With the resour…"

"And multiple shots were heard," insisted Lestrade, cutting across Parker, and turning back to Holmes. "And multiple wounds were found on the main part of body. And there are five bullets in this vial."

A grave look came over Holmes's face. "I have known suicides and killings where the victim needed multiple shots to be finished off. It is one of the most gruesome part of finding a body that has come to a violent end."

Lestrade turned to me.

"Dr Watson, can you imagine a case where multiple shots were required to finish off a killing?"

"I am an old soldier," I said making sure as far as I could that I only said things that were true. "I have seen a killing with a small weapon where several shots were required to finish the job and it is conceivable that that was the case here." I paused, wondering, as I caught on to Holmes's *modus operandi*.

"In a suicide?" asked Lestrade with disbelief written on his features.

"If that is the weapon used," I replied, feeling some unsteadiness in my voice, "it is very small and it is conceivable…", but Lestrade came to my rescue before I said anything more.

"And what of the two men who were all but caught red-handed, Mr Holmes?"

"Here is my theory of what happened, Inspector," said Holmes with the air of someone summing up something that should, in reality, be obvious to everyone. "When you came to see us at Baker Street about Milverton's death, you said that he was known to have held papers which he used for blackmailing purposes and that all the papers in Milverton's safe were burnt. You speculated that the criminals probably were men of good position, whose sole object was to prevent social exposure."

"That is so."

"I suspect that Milverton surprised these men as they burnt the contents of his safe. It is hard to get into Milverton's mind in such a situation. But a man such as he would always have been armed and may have felt there was no hope for him once his means of blackmailing people had been destroyed. Or maybe he had a twinge of conscience at what he had done. I am sure that Milverton would have made sure that his fire-arm was easily concealable, so it had to be a small weapon like this one. With his life's work destroyed, he might have turned the gun on himself."

"You seriously think that that would drive him to suicide?"

"I have no other theory to explain how the weapon which killed him might have been found in a dark corner of the room where his body was found. The criminals who escaped would have had no reason to discard their weapon at all and every reason not to. As is so often the case, once you exclude the impossible, whatever remains *must* be the truth."

"So has any crime been committed at all?"

"Breaking and entering as these two men did to get into Milverton's safe is a serious offence," said Holmes thoughtfully. "But if you should identify these criminals, I am not sure whether you want to bring a case of theft where the objects stolen were documents, the exposure of any of which would blacken the reputation of some of the most eminent names in the country. It would almost be seen as a punishment for those who were the victims of blackmail. And the victims would have had no justice as the blackmailer has put himself beyond the reach of the law."

"So is there anything to be gained in continuing this investigation?"

"I have offered you my theory of suicide which will explain Milverton's death. And you have had five days, footprints, and a good description to track these two men down whom you describe as criminals and yet you seem to have seen neither hide nor hair of either of them. And in the end you have found no evidence that a woman was involved at all. Your pointed heel has turned out to be a corner of a table and none of the domestic staff have mentioned a third person being on the scene and any tracks she might have made a few days ago will be long gone by now if they were ever there. I suspect if your investigation goes on much longer, someone else will come up with my theory, and you will be accused of wasting police resources."

"But Miss Brown, whom I saw this morning, gave me a description of a stranger whom she used to – uh – see in the grounds of the house. Tall, well-spoken, with a missing front tooth. He may be the associate of the thick-set man we so nearly apprehended."

His eyes wondered from Holmes to me and back again. I could feel my heart pounding in my chest as I thought he was about to say something but before Lestrade could speak, up piped Parker again.

"There's more budgets cuts coming our way, Inspector. I can feel it in my bones. It would not do to be seen wasting police time at a time when everything is so tight."

I suspect the sergeant was anxious to ensure a swift end to the case so that that the apparent deficiencies of his search of the room might be overlooked. Whatever the reason, Lestrade gave him a hunted look. Then he strode from the room with the air of a man whose mind was made up. Parker, Holmes, and I followed. As he made his way through the hallway, the butler approached him and said, "The staff are all at readiness to help you with your investigation, Inspector."

"I have no need to see them, Broderick," replied Lestrade. "I am happy to say I have been able to solve the case to my full satisfaction without the need to interrogate them. There is no getting past me, and in the end my investigations revealed the matter as a most simple one. My officers will remove your master's body as soon as possible and show the same discretion as when it was brought in."

"Very good, sir. Mr Milverton was a most kindly employer, and everyone will be pleased when the matter of his death has been resolved. Could I have your confirmation that the staff are now free to go about their business."

"On that last matter, Roderick, you may tell your staff that that is indeed the case. No one here is suspected of involvement of any kind in this matter."

"That is most excellent news."

We were back at Baker Street and sitting by the fireside before Holmes said another word.

"The case was, as Lestrade observed, a most simple one. Thus, providing a plausible alternative to the manifest facts was extremely difficult. My first step was to contact the lady who carried out the killing. With my name, I got an appointment easily, and I taxed her with the killing."

"You blackmailed her?"

"I had learnt the art of blackmail from seeing a master in action, and I am pleased I turned it to a good cause at last. I got her pistol which you saw. And I observed that the lady had gaps in her domestic staff which might not otherwise have been apparent to her. She was thus eager to engage Miss Brown whose name I proposed and whose address I gave her. She wrote to Miss Brown offering her a position as her housemaid with an immediate start and this meant that Miss Brown would not be at the house when I went there with you to see Lestrade."

"Did she not have misgivings about engaging an employee of Mr Milverton."

"My hold over the lady was such," replied Holmes, slightly austerely, "that she was in no position to turn down any of my suggestions."

And that was that. Not a word more would Holmes say about the matter just past but a few months later a letter arrived addressed to me. This was not one of the fashionable missives my friend was wont to receive but a letter on simple stationery in a hand probably not used to writing very often.

Dear Dr Watson

I wanted to thank you for your patience with me at my time of need. It can't have been much of a pleasure listening to me bleating on about a man who I now realise was never going to do and I am sure you must have had that opinion too but were far too kind to say so. Just after I last saw you, out of the blue, a lady wrote to offer me a situation

– the same duties at Appledore Towers but paying a good third more. After a few months in service, I was able to prevail on my mistress to offer a situation to my former admirer, Mr Caldwell, as head-gardener.

My first love was always a much better choice for me than Mr Escott could ever have been and, to please me, Mr Caldwell has even taken up smoking from a clay pipe like Mr Escott used to.

He and I are to be wed next week so everything has turned out for the better in the end.

With my kindest regards and renewed thanks for your kindness,

Agatha Brown (soon to be Caldwell).

A Christmas Carol

And yet there is so much about Holmes and me that is unexplained. Why was my wound first described as being in the shoulder and then in the leg, what caused Holmes to fire bullets at the wall to honour our queen with the letters VR, and where does Stanley Hopkins spring from when none of the earlier chronicles I allowed to be published in my lifetime make any mention of him? As my reader may imagine, there must be a reason to redact the background to matters of such moment and the events that I now describe will make it obvious to the reader why their publication must wait until long after my death.

It was on Christmas morning 1886 that Holmes glanced to the window with a look of long-suffering. "I fear," said he, "that while on any day I find the activities of my fellow man superficial beyond mere ennui, it is at Christmas that this superficiality is the most unbearable of all."

It was not as though the days leading up to Christmas Day 1886 had been devoid of activity. We had taken Jevans, the poisoner, as well as Perkiss, who specialism was the garrotte. "Crimes without refinement and rather *infra dig* or beneath my level," Holmes had opined loftily at these cases' conclusion. The same could not be said about Thurley, whose way of despatching his victims was a matter of such horror and subtlety that details of his methods, capture, and prosecution are, for reasons my reader will understand, beyond even the scope of writings such as these, which are not intended for publication until long after my death.

It had been Inspector Lestrade who had gained most from these early successes in Holmes's Baker Street career as my friend declined to have his name associated with any of them and thus our ferrety-faced visitor had earned all the credit. "I made my way up through the ranks," declared Lestrade proudly one day, before asking for Holmes's help him solve another case, "and now royal security is in my remit. And I have a team of six men to support me on this. Who knows where I will get to next?"

At this festive season our landlady, Mrs Hudson, had betaken herself to the house of her daughter, Mrs Turner, and Holmes and I had been left with victuals sufficient for the first two days of Christmas as the rest of the Baker Street staff had been given both Christmas Day and Boxing Day off.

On that Christmas morning Holmes had taken advantage of the absence from the house of anyone but me to conduct a chemical experiment which was so loud as to banish any sense of heavenly peace and so pungent as to banish any temptation to partake even of the figgy pudding that Mrs Hudson had brought out before her departure. My friend's experiment involved noxious gases and electrical appliances and at random intervals the air was rent by loud crackles as livid blue currents flashed blindingly between two metallic balls. As if the battering my senses were subject to from Holmes's experiment was insufficient, the merry playing of a barrel organ operated by what I assumed from his wooden leg was an old soldier on the street below, added to the cacophony. The melodies of *The Holly and the Ivy*, *Good King Wenceslas*, and *The Twelve Days of Christmas* rang out loudly even though the window of our first-floor sitting-room was kept tight shut, and it was sound from below which had provoked Holmes's initial remark. I went to the window and noted that the grinder had a monkey on his device and the animal gibbered as it danced to the familiar tunes. It was no surprise to see the old soldier doing a roaring trade with the many passers-by on this festive morning and I could see we would have to put up with his noisy presence for some time.

I returned to my seat by the fireside. A few minutes more and there was a brief intermission in the music – when I glanced into the street again I saw the barrel-organist fossicking in the mechanisms of his machine – and it was at this moment that I heard the bell ring.

In the absence of any staff, and with Holmes fully engaged, I realised it would have to be I who would have to go to see who it was. "Too early in the day and too late in the season for carol-singers," was the thought that occurred to me on the stair, "though who else might be calling us on the morning of the first day of Christmas?"

In retrospect, it should perhaps not have come as a surprise that I found Inspector Lestrade on the doorstep.

"I'd been ringing for ages, Dr Watson," grumbled he. "I thought you and Mr Holmes had gone away."

I brought him up into our little sitting room which was now full of pungent fumes and the barrel-organ player in the street started up again.

"Mr Holmes," began Lestrade, spluttering slightly as the noxious gases caught his lungs and raising his voice to make himself heard above the din from the street below. "I am sorry to have disturbed you on this day of all days. I have a matter for your attention."

"My experiment is at a stage where it can be paused," replied Holmes, somewhat to my relief. He offered both Lestrade and me a cigar, took one himself, and we sat down. I drew heavily on the cigar, pleased that its sweet scent mitigated the reek from Holmes's experiment and, as we took our seats, I noted the player from the street seemed to be moving on as the clangour of his organ started to fade into the distance.

"We yesterday arrested a criminal who is well known to us at the Yard," continued Lestrade. "O'Flaherty is part of a gang that specialises in breaking into shops and then selling their booty at markets. His gang was spotted yesterday breaking into a toyshop on Tottenham Court Road. A party of policemen was despatched, and O'Flaherty was caught red-handed though other members of the gang escaped."

Holmes's face fell and I could see that he felt that breaking and entering was another case that fell below his level.

"There had been similar cases in the area, and we were going to charge O'Flaherty with several crimes,"

Lestrade carried on. "I think it was in the hope of only being charged with the Tottenham Road offence, but, under questioning, O'Flaherty divulged to us a Fenian or Irish plot to assassinate our Queen."

"But there must be rumours of such plots all the time," objected Holmes. "This country is surrounded by people and countries who wish it ill. You have not come here on this day and disturbed me from my chemical analysis to consult with me on an act of minor larceny and vague rumours of an assassination plot."

Lestrade was not to be put off.

"That is so. After the revellers of midnight mass have retired, almost all business premises in London and across the country are shut on Christmas night. One of the few exceptions to this is the telegraph office on the corner of Trafalgar Square by Pall Mall. This is open twenty-four hours a day, seven days a week, three-hundred-and-sixty-five days a year. This is convenient for the residents of Belgravia – mainly royalty and senior politicians – who can still send telegrams round the world irrespective of the time of day or the day of the week. Indeed, this first day of Christmas is one of this office's busiest times of year as this is the only place in the country from which messages can be sent."

"Pray continue," said Holmes, and I could see from his suddenly alert expression that the introduction of a telegraph office to Lestrade's exposition had aroused his attention.

"There is a special deposit box where messages and money can be left for the message to be transmitted without the customer and the clerk ever setting eyes on each other. Although it is not a matter that is widely publicised, telegram operators are briefed to look out for unusual telegrams. Clearly this is not fail-safe because of the volume of such correspondence but the attention of the Trafalgar Square telegram office was drawn to the following message. The telegram was sent for the attention of a Mr Zaine O'Malley to be collected at the main telegraph office in Boston in the United States."

He handed Holmes a piece of paper on which was written.

25.12.1886

01.25

RETTP TTEETPTR EE PEAIGPIDA AANAAT

"The first word consists of five letters and has the same letter twice in as its third and fourth characters. This is consistent with it being the word Queen and T standing for E," said Lestrade. "And the spacing of letter is consistent with this being a substitution code – so where one letter stands for another."

"If it is a substitution code, how many words of two letters are there with two identical letters like the third word of this message."

55

"I have only just received this message, Mr Holmes, so there are limits..."

"The only two letter word, apart from exclamations, that I can think of consisting of two identical letters is "Aa" which is a type of floating lava. And the last two letters of the fourth word are the same as the first two words of the fifth."

"It is for your help that I am here Mr Holmes..."

"In English," continued Holmes, his eyes half-closed and addressing the room rather than Lestrade, "there are many words that end with double E, double S, and double L but none that start with double S or double L although there are many words in Welsh that start with a double LL. If A is E, then we have one word which ends with a double E and another which starts with a double E and the only words that do the latter relate to 'eeriness' and 'eels,' which would seem have as little relevance to Her Majesty as floating lava."

"I came here from your help, Mr Holmes. At the moment you are merely illustrating the difficulties that I face."

To me Holmes had slipped into his own world as he had talked about the code but now he focused on Lestrade.

"I cannot, I fear, Inspector, help with such limited data. You are asking me to make bricks without straw. And yet there are depths here I..."

"I was going to say, Mr Holmes, that O'Flaherty is in the cells at the Marylebone Magistrates Court around the corner from here. I was going to ask you if you would join me in interrogating him."

I could see that Holmes's interest was piqued, and I had good reason to want to escape the confines of our room and in less time than it takes to say the foregoing, we were on our way.

"What can you tell me about O'Flaherty," Holmes asked Lestrade, as we turned the corner from Baker Street.

"As I indicated to you, Mr Holmes, O'Flaherty is a career criminal who has passed through our hands several times. I would describe him as unintelligent, unreliable, and uneducated – alas a common description of so many of the criminals who pass through our hands. Accordingly, it is highly debateable how much weight can be placed on anything he says."

"And why is he in the cells at Marylebone Magistrates Court rather than in a police cell?"

"The normal prison cells are full of people who have over-indulged themselves celebrating the season. We often make use of the court cells at this time of year as the courts themselves are not in use."

"Can the American police not help us identify this O'Malley?"

"I fear, Mr Holmes, that getting the American police to help us at Scotland Yard is difficult under most circumstances. To get the Boston police to give us information on someone masterminding a Fenian Plot is quite impossible."

We were soon at Marylebone Magistrates Court.

"The cells are underneath the courtroom," said Lestrade as he got the keys from the duty officer, and we went down some stairs.

We found O'Flaherty's cell empty.

The bars of the cell's high little window had been sawn through and wrenched out.

"He must have been sprung," cried Lestrade. "He will have been searched before he was taken down here and a tool or several tools must have been used to force the bars."

"That can only imply that some grave matter is afoot," said Holmes. "A criminal of no importance would not be sprung by an outsider and an organization whose ambitions are limited to burglary would not have the means to spring him."

We were just about to leave the courthouse when a messenger dashed up to Lestrade and handed him an envelope.

"It is another message in code!" exclaimed Lestrade as he opened it. "No!" he said, looking again, "it is two messages."

I set them out below:

25.12.1886

02.23

DRUUS TEAST AA PTSTAESTLTE

AS WAIEST TTD

25.12.1186

02.57

WD AATES RAAE PA NTSOATP TA AUS TE

Holmes looked at the two messages.

"These are deep waters indeed," he said after examining them briefly but intently. "I note that the second message again has a five-letter word with the third and the fourth the same which suggests Queen. But whereas in the first message the five-letter code read RETTP, here it is DRUUS."

"There are many other five letter words which repeat the third and fourth letter," said Lestrade. "'Curry', or 'Steep' are just two examples."

"You may be right, Inspector, but it is hard to think of a seven-word message using 'Curry' or 'Steep' or any other word with that pattern of letters which would require encryption."

"Or 'shoot'," shot back Lestrade, who had, I think, been slightly nettled by Holmes's dismissive tone since he had first raised the matter that he wanted my friend to investigate.

And for once Holmes had no response.

"Could two different codes be being used?" I asked.

"That may be so," replied Holmes gloomily, "and indeed is the likeliest explanation. But having two codes rather one that merely doubles our problem. Or three, if it is three codes. And we have not the data to exclude that possibility."

"Why do you think the time of the message is in each case put at its head?" I asked. "The time of despatch is included on any telegraph so that the receiver knows when it was transmitted."

"I fear that that detail makes this matter more troubling still," said Holmes, soberly. "It implies that there are multiple messages – indeed, many more than we know about – and that it is important that the receiver knows the order in which they were written as information is updated. If this is a substitution code, and the pattern of the letters suggests nothing else, it is of a complexity I have not seen before."

"And yet the Inspector here described O'Flaherty as being uneducated, unintelligent, and unreliable. Would a person answering such a description be involved with a gang using a code of this sophistication?"

The question hung in air as Holmes turned on his heel without farewell. I followed him back to Baker Street. I assume Lestrade returned to Scotland Yard.

We had left the window of our sitting room open, so the smell of chemicals had almost gone. The atmosphere was improved atmosphere further when Holmes lit another cigar while I lit my pipe. Holmes was in no mood for conversation, and he sat in his chair, apart from one moment when he went to the window and asked the barrel organ player, who had resumed his station beneath our window, to move on. He had not stirred from his seat when at four o'clock a messenger delivered a note from Lestrade.

"Mr Holmes

I regret to inform you that we have been unable to find any trace of O'Flaherty although urgent efforts to find him continue.

George Lestrade"

The note filled Holmes with more gloom.

"In other words," he said, "Lestrade has no idea of the whereabouts of the only person of interest in this case. And he had had him in his custody. And we know nothing more about this plot than that it seems to progress through messages in a code we are completely unable to decrypt so I am no further forward than he."

It was at this grave moment that he got his pistol out and fired bullets at the wall, not stopping until the outline of VR had been traced on it, and rendering our room a cauldron of sulphurous fumes and hot metal.

He addressed no further word to me that first day of Christmas and I eventually retired to my room. When I arose the next morning it was to find Holmes occupying the small part of the table not taken up by the instruments of his experiment from the previous day as he sat hunched over the pieces of paper with the coded messages on them.

My heart sank when I saw the look of gloom on his face.

"Let us to Lestrade and see if there have been any developments. I make no progress. It galls me to say it, but he cannot have been less successful than I."

We went down onto Baker Street and were lucky to be able to hail one of the few Hansom cabs running on Boxing Day. In another twenty minutes we were in Lestrade's office in Scotland Yard at Whitehall where we found the Inspector sat looking as gloomy faced as Holmes had done at Baker Street as he stared at the same three coded messages.

"What can you tell us, Inspector, about the Queen's movements over the next few days?" Holmes asked at last. "And what additional security measures have you taken?"

"Well, with my responsibility for the Queen's security, you're certainly asking the right person, Mr Holmes," said Lestrade, pulling himself up proudly to his full height. "While, in the circumstances we face, half-confidences would be absurd, I would beg you not to disclose the information I am about to give to you to anyone else. I would undoubtedly be in hot water if it got out that I had given information about the Queen's movements to an outsider."

I think Holmes was surprised that Lestrade saw the need to make this request at all, but he merely nodded, and Lestrade continued.

"The Queen spent the morning of the Eve of Christmas at Windsor and returned to Buckingham Palace from there by Royal Train arriving at Waterloo station at three o'clock in the afternoon – so in other words, the day before yesterday, the 24th of December. It is customary for her to spend this first day of Christmas in London with her family – children and grand-children, the Prince of Wales, Edward Albert, will have been present. Being in London makes it easier for people to come and see her as well as for members of her court to see their families, but the Queen generally much prefers the comforts of her country estates."

"Which one will she go to?"

"Sandringham in Norfolk, one hundred miles to the north-east of London, is her preference. The Royal Train was moved overnight from Waterloo through the suburbs of West London to the sidings of Kentish Town station three miles to the north of St Pancras. Railway staff were paid what I imagine to be an extravagant level of overtime on Christmas Day to make the train ready to go down to St Pancras Station today – the second day of Christmas or Boxing Day. The train will take her to Wolferton, which is the closest station to the estate."

"But if Sandringham is in Norfolk, would the train not go from Liverpool Street?

"The monarch is normally barred from the City of London and accordingly her train is routed from St Pancras to Norfolk via Tottenham."

"And what will happen next?"

"The Queen will stay at Sandringham until the start of the New Year. She will then return once more from

Wolferton Station to St Pancras and go to Buckingham Palace where she will stay until the twelve days of Christmas are up. She will next go to Osborne House on the Isle of Wight after the Christmas season is over and there are no further plans for her at present until her Golden Jubilee is celebrated next year. As you will be aware, Queen Victoria is now sixty-seven and has been leading a life withdrawn from the public eye for many years, so it is rare to schedule anything more than a few weeks into the future. Her Golden Jubilee celebrations planned for next year are an exception to this."

"And what security measures are in place to protect her?"

"At all times the Queen is the subject of tight security, but this is easier to enforce when she is in the interior of one of the royal palaces or in the Royal Train than when she is *en route* between the Royal Train and a residence. Thus, Christmas time is an obvious time for an assassin to strike as this is one of the few times of the year when she is making reasonably predictable moves from place to place. For her journey from Waterloo station to Buckingham Palace which I referred to, she travelled in a closed, unmarked carriage with sidesmen at each door and unmarked carriages as an escort front and back. A by-stander might therefore realise that the escorted carriage he sees is carrying a personage of importance, but he will not be aware of quite how great the importance."

"Pray continue."

"The same procedures will be followed for the journey to St Pancras tomorrow and for the journey from

Wolferton Station to her house on the Sandringham estate and, again, when she returns to London at the start of the New Year."

"And what route will be taken through London?"

"The direct route from Buckingham Palace to St Pancras is clockwise on the west and north sides of Trafalgar Square, north up the Charing Cross Road, across Oxford Street, up the Tottenham Court Road, and then east the along the Euston Road. As I indicated to you, the Queen's unmarked carriage is escorted front and back by security carriages. The Queen's regular coachman, Martlet, is under instructions to follow the front security carriage and only, Graham, the driver of this security carriage, knows the route to be taken which was the one specified in the foregoing. And it is I, in my capacity as the Queen's protector, who specifies the route to take."

At that moment, there was a knock on the door.

"Message for you from the Strand Telegraph Office, sir," said a young constable, handing Lestrade an envelope.

"Thank you, Hopkins," said Lestrade. "The Strand Telegraph Office is one that closes on Christmas night but is open all night every other day of the year," said Lestrade.

My reader will be unsurprised to see that that the envelope it contained two further coded messages.

26.12.1886

03.12

HETTNNR HRRHNNRETE TTHTRE TU UEN

and

26.12.1886

03.27

UOTFTHRTO TWRTOE RETONNR ROSTT OE

USUUENETE HSROU OE ERTUSN OE

"The distribution of words again implies a substitution code," said Holmes, "and yet the third word of this fourth message again appears to have the same two letters at the beginning – although this time with T rather than with A in the first message - with all the implausibilities that that implies."

He noted down the two new messages. "Let us walk back to Baker Street, good Watson," he said, addressing no further word to Lestrade. "Maybe some fresh air will give me some ideas. And if not fresh air, maybe exposure to the tobacco-smoke laden atmosphere of Baker Street will do the trick."

We walked in silence for some time.

Then, as we were crossing crossed Manchester Square, a thought seemed to strike Holmes and he sat down on a bench.

"Let us look at these five messages in summary," said he, laying them out on his knee. "By the length of the divisions of characters, it must be a code where the letters we have here represent letters of a word. But look at the frequency of the letters that represent the code."

With striking rapidity, he tabulated the frequencies for me, and I reproduce the table he wrote into his notebook below.

Message 1		Message 2		Message 3		Message 4		Message 5		Message 6	
7	A	6	A	8	A	5	R	9	O	15	N
4	P	6	S	3	S	5	N	8	R	10	I
6	E	4	E	3	E	7	T	10	T	9	M
7	T	9	T	5	T	5	E	9	E	15	S

	Message 1	Message 2	Message 3	Message 4	Message 5	Message 6
Letters in message	31	34	27	28	53	71
Number of characters covered by most common four letters	24	25	19	22	36	49
%	77.4%	73.5%	70.4%	78.6%	67.9%	69.0%

"Look Watson," said he, "in each message, four letters represent at least two thirds of the characters."

"What is the significance of that?" I asked.

"You try to construct an unencrypted message of more than a few characters where four dominate to such an extent. It is an impossible task."

Perhaps I looked a little blank, but my friend started to write again.

"I just said, 'It is an impossible task'. That has twenty-four letters, but the dominant ones - S, I, A, and T - occur four times, four times, twice, and twice. Twelve times in total so only half the population of letters. Or take that saying of mine you like to quote, 'It is quite a three-pipe problem". That has twenty-six letters and the most frequently used characters, E, I, T, and P occur four times, thrice, thrice, and thrice - so only thirteen times in total."

"So what is your inference from that?"

"I have done no more than observe, I am not yet at the stage to infer. You have done no more than see the letters, but you have not yet made even an observation."

"You have merely reordered the problem," I retorted. "You have not solved it. And you are not even close to solving it."

"This problem must be solvable," said my friend, and into his voice came a note of desperation I had never heard before.

There was a silence and I ventured.

"Have you given any thought about what information the message might be trying to convey."

My friend suddenly became animated.

"By Jove! Watson, you've got it!" He glanced at his watch which was showing ten minutes to ten. "Come! There is not a moment to lose!"

My friend sprang from our bench and ran south down Duke Street before turning east into Oxford Street. I was left toiling in his wake, hampered by the wound from a Jazail bullet in my shoulder – a remnant of the Afghan campaign of six years previously – which made my arm throb agonisingly at every sudden movement. By the time I had got to the corner of Oxford Street, Holmes was out of sight. In the end I turned and made a slow walk back to Baker Street. The sun had come out and it was for December a pleasant day. As I was in no hurry, and, eager to get the last of the gases from Holmes's experiments of the previous day out of my lungs, I took am extended stroll through Regents Park before arriving at 221 from the north side.

When I arrived, the organ-grinder was again churning out the last verse of the *Twelve Days of Christmas* and then switched to performing the eight verses of *While Shepherds Watched their Flocks by Night.* I was also unsurprised to see that waiting outside the house beside the organ grinder was Lestrade.

"I'd been hoping to see Mr Holmes," he said, looking slightly disappointed when he saw that I was on my own.

We went upstairs.

"It looks like there's been a leak of information about the Queen's movements," Lestrade said when we sat in our siting-room. "There was an attempt to cause a traffic jam where the Queen's carriage was passing. A man was arrested when he caused an obstruction at the exit to Charing Cross Road from Trafalgar Square. That's the route I told you and Mr Holmes the Queen's carriage would take. The man who caused the obstruction lay down in the roadway. It caused a huge build-up of traffic. The Queen's coach and its escort were caught up in it and would have made an easy target for an assassin."

"Might it not simply be a coincidence with a man in drink – not unusual at this time of year. Or someone who has lost their reason. Surely no one in a normal state of mind would lie in the roadway at such a busy point."

"That is what I would like Mr Holmes for. The royal party had to be diverted up Grey's Inn Road to St Pancras, and we had no protection for them there. We had stationed extra officers on Charing Cross Road and Tottenham Court Road to make sure that nothing untoward happened to the royal party. Going by the route they did, anyone could have got them. From an official point of view, this looks terrible. I had gone home – I live not far from Baker Street, which is why I am such a regular visitor here – having spent all night trying to crack the code and a messenger brought me the news."

"What is to happen now?"

"The offender is in the cells at Scotland Yard, and I came straight here was hoping I could persuade Mr Holmes to come and join me in interrogating our suspect."

I had no desire to spend any more time than I had to on my own in the sitting room with the barrel-organ grinding away relentlessly outside and I asked more in hope than in expectation, "Might I join you? You may need the insights of a medical man for a matter like this if it is a matter of your suspect's sanity. I have been reading up on the lates…"

"God bless you Dr Watson. It can't harm if you come. At least I am not breaching any confidences with you as you already know everything. How information about the Queen's whereabouts got out is sure to be subject of an investigation. I suppose if I can't have Mr Holmes," he continued as we walked down the stairs, "or if I can't have the organ-grinder," he said looking at the street musician who again seemed to have become a fixture outside our house, "I can at least see what I can do with the organ-grinder's monkey."

I was not sure quite what to make of this last remark, but let it pass, and in less than half an hour we were at Scotland Yard.

"The Chief wants to see you, sir," said the desk sergeant when Lestrade and I arrived at the Yard.

"The Chief!" exclaimed Lestrade. "I would not expect the Chief to be here on Boxing Day." He turned to me, "I am not allowed even to disclose to you the Chief's name. And I have a prisoner to s…"

"Lestrade," boomed a voice, from a corridor leading off to the side.

"Yes, sir," replied Lestrade with a meekness that was entirely uncustomary of him.

I did not have to have particularly sharp hearing to follow what happened next as Lestrade's Chief did not

71

trouble to close the door of his office and made no attempt to lower his voice.

"The man," I heard, "who was arrested at the junction of Charing Cross Road and Trafalgar Square was your friend, Mr Sherlock Holmes. He has found out the itinerary of the Queen and that leak of top-secret data can only have come from you. What were you thinking of?"

The door through which I was listening to Lestrade's dressing down was slammed shut at this point so I could not hear any more but shortly afterwards a woebegone Lestrade returned to where I was waiting in the Scotland Yard reception.

"You will have heard," he said, "what the Chief said before I closed his door. I have been demoted to the ranks."

"What about Mr Holmes?" I asked.

"The Chief has said that if you can stand bail for him, he can be released. But he will be subject to a guard until he appears in court tomorrow and agrees to be bound over to keep the peace."

I had to pay over all the cash that Holmes and I had on us. Then for the second time that Boxing Day, Holmes and I set off towards Baker Street but this time it was in the ignominious confines of a police cart accompanied by the young constable, Hopkins, whom I referred to above.

"I have been instructed to remain with you until I am relieved, sir," said Hopkins.

Holmes was as relaxed about the situation as I was uncomfortable with it, and he chuckled at Hopkins's remark.

"I see no reason why you should not sit with us in our little sitting room, Constable," he said as we arrived at Baker Street. "I can assure you that I will not seek to escape your gaze. You will be more comfortable there than standing guard at the street door."

I was unsurprised when Holmes focused on cracking the code the instant we were back in our sitting room.

"It was your comment, Watson, that made me lie down to block the entrance to Charing Cross Road. You asked if we might not try to decipher the coded messages by thinking what they might be saying in their messages. Look at this!" and he laid out the fifth message. "If OE is Rd, the abbreviation of road, then before it we have the right number of letters for Charing Cross, Tottenham Court, and Euston."

As usual when my friend made his inferences I wondered why I had not spotted what he had said in the message below.

UOTFTHRTO TWRTOE RETONNR ROSTT OE

USUUENETE HSROU OE ERTUSN OE

"But if your theory is correct," I countered, "then E stands for the D of the abbreviated form of Road, and for G, and for E itself."

"Then some characters are representing more than one letter. Otherwise, the message would not give a good sense. That was the inference I should have made yesterday from the distribution of the letters that I observed."

"Perhaps you could explain."

"This is a substitution code, but it probably is a code which refers to the position of letters in a target text. If the text used for the encryption has the same letter twice within twenty-six letters, then the same letter will represent more than one letter of unencrypted text."

I think Holmes saw my blank look and Holmes expanded on his thesis.

"This morning I noted that the leading four characters of each code text constituted over two-thirds of the total population. I pointed out that in the phrases 'it is an impossible task,' and 'It is quite a three-pipe problem', the leading four characters constituted no more than just over half of the message. But look what happens if the letters of 'It is quite a three-pipe problem,' which has the advantage of having exactly twenty-six letters are used to code 'It is an impossible task.'"

Holmes draw another peculiar table which I replicate below:

MESSAGE	TARGET
A	I
B	T
C	I
D	S
E	Q
F	U
G	I

H	T
I	E
J	A
K	T
L	H
M	R
N	E
O	E
P	P
Q	I
R	P
S	E
T	P
U	R
V	O
W	B
X	L
Y	E
Z	M

"If you use 'It is quite a three-pipe problem,' as a substitute code for the alphabet," he went on, "and then use that code to encrypt, 'It is an impossible task,' you get this."

IT IS AN IMPOSSIBLE TASK

EP EE IE ERPEEEETHQ PIET

"This coding concentrates the most common letters in the alphabet. Here, in twenty-six letters, E appears no fewer than ten times as it represents A, N, O, S, and Y.

"But surely having cracked one message, the code used by the Fenians should be easy to crack. Have you applied your methodology to another of the messages."

"Ah, there's the rub. Let us take the message I think referred to roads in London – Charing Cross Road, Tottenham Court Road, and Euston Road."

He set it out as below and I highlight the three roads my friend identified:

UOTFTHRTO TWRTOE RETONNR ROSTT **OE**

USUUENETE HSROU **OE** ERTUSN **OE**

O is the R and E is the D of the abbreviation Rd of Road, then E is the opening E of Euston Road and both the H and the M of Tottenham Court Road.

"If I apply the letter I have identified above to another message, let us see what happens.

HETTNNR HRRHNNTETE TTHTRE TU UEN

H is one of the letters we have not decrypted but if E is D, and T is the A of Charing Cross Road, then, we have a word with a D followed by two A's. That is an unlikely basis for success."

"Does this not prove that there are multiple codes?"

"Self-evidently so. And even if we have largely solved one, that does not solve the others, and we have no means of knowing why and how they switch from one code to another. And this will not work for the trap I have in mind to set for the conspirators."

Hopkins had been following our discussions at the door but at this point we heard a ring on the door.

"It's two o'clock and I'm at the end of my shift. I'll ask my relief to come up. And," he said, with an ear cocked to the street, "our organ grinder is at the second day of Christmas. It all seems to…"

"By Jove, Hopkins!" exclaimed Holmes. "You've got it! I congratulate you."

I thought Holmes would give us a detailed explanation of the code.

Instead, he perused the five coded messages he had laid out before him before issuing one of his familiar low chuckles of contentment.

He then proceeded to write what I could only read over his shoulder two notes in the code – or, given Holmes's previous remarks, in one or more of the of the codes.

I reproduce his messages below:

26.12.1886
07.19

NN SININIW SM SMIEMI SGM MW SANNSE ENV NIGSMI NE WMGNN GS ESMMWGEINE GS GS WSNSNIG SSIN

and

26.12.1886
08.43

GKEHNKGAS EE SVLGEDKL KM LTN
KSMKGH SE ELH IMKKISIVGW SE

He then wrote a separate note before turning Hopkins.

"As you are now off-duty, are you able to help me privately, Hopkins?" he asked.

The young constable thought for a second.

"Well, I suppose there's no reason not to, sir."

"Very well," said Holmes. "Could I ask you to take these two messages to the Trafalgar Square telegraph office and despatch them. And then could you take this other missive to Lestrade at his home address."

Hopkins departed to be replaced by a new constable and it was not until the twenty-seventh of December that Holmes had appeared in court, paid a substantial fine for obstruction of the Queen's highway, and a further amount to be bound over, that we were free of a constant police presence. When we returned to Baker Street after the humiliation of my friend's appearance in court, I expected Holmes to focus on cracking the code. Instead, he returned to his noxious experiments. The air was once more filled with pungent fumes and rent by deafening crackles, and the only relief was that the organ grinder at our window seemed to have left us permanently.

It was not until half-past-eleven on the morning of the thirtieth of December that Holmes addressed a word to me.

"I cannot help but feel, good Watson, that I have done Inspector Lestrade –"

" – Constable Lestrade now," I reminded my friend, who ignored my interjection.

"A disservice. I have therefore arranged a minor jollification for him and his colleagues this lunchtime at the Rose pub at the junction of Bloomsbury Street and New Oxford Street. Would you like to join us?"

Such a gesture seemed so out of keeping with my friend's normal austere habits that it was in a daze that I agreed. By two o'clock a somewhat rueful-looking Lestrade, his six colleagues, Holmes, and I were gathered at the Rose. It was another unseasonably mild day and we stood outside the pub. I noted that barriers had been set down at the road junction to enable roadworks to take place and although no work was taking place, the presence of the signs meant that the traffic went past at a crawl.

Suddenly Lestrade cried, "Look men! There's O'Flaherty loitering at the opposite corner! And some of his gang there too."

I have often quoted Holmes's criticisms of the intelligence of the police force but never in all the cases I undertook with my friend did I see a lack of courage or sense of duty in the Scotland Yard officers I encountered. To a man they put down their drinks and stormed across the road. I am not sure that as a man bound over to keep the peace, Holmes should have joined them, and my wounded shoulder made any involvement by me perhaps even more unwise, but the game was afoot.

My lack of prudence was brought home to me as I heard a shot being fired and an instant later I felt as though someone had put a white-hot poker to my leg.

As I sank to the ground, I saw a furious melee before me, and another man fell to the ground as a second shot was discharged.

My next clear recollection was to wake up in St Bartholomew's Hospital to find Holmes at my bedside and my leg encased in a huge bandage.

"It has all worked out splendidly," said my friend breezily.

"I am not sure I quite see it that way," I replied, the pain from my leg seeming to blot out everything else.

With a solicitousness that was unusual for him, Holmes lit a cigarette for me, and in the end I was able to prop myself up on my arm to and draw on it.

"I had laid a trap for O'Flaherty and his gang," said my friend triumphantly. "And they walked straight into it. It has been a complete triumph for Lestrade."

For an instant the news that Holmes had apparently solved his case blotted out the pain from my leg.

Holmes fished out of his pocket two slips of paper each of which bore one of the messages he had asked Hopkins to take to the telegraph office.

"The code being used," said he, "was in fact a simple substitution code and you had spotted the clue to cracking it in the earliest stages of the investigation."

"I?" I exclaimed.

"Yes. You asked why the time of the writing of the message was included on each message."

"But you said that was to indicate the order in which messages had been written and postulated that there may be many more messages than we were aware of."

"Yes, it was not until the excellent Hopkins commented that he was being relieved at two o'clock as the barrel organist played the second day of the *Twelve Days of Christmas* that an alternative and as it turns out a correct reason occurred to me."

I must still have looked blank, and Holmes clicked with impatience.

"Good Watson, if you have multiple substitution codes, the recipient needs to know which one is being used for each message. The text being used for the codes was *The Twelve Days of Christmas.* The time on each message indicated which verse was forming the basis of the substitution code. So, the first verse referring to 'A Partridge in a Pear Tree' gives a code table as follows." And Holmes set out the table below:

A	A
B	P
C	A
D	R
E	T
F	R

G	I
H	D
I	G
J	E
K	I
L	N
M	A
N	P
O	E
P	A
Q	R
R	T
S	R
T	E
U	E
V	A
W	P
X	A
Y	R
Z	T

The first message was marked as having been written at 1.25 and so the cypher would be derived from the partridge in a pear tree of the first day of Christmas.

Using the code gave me:

QUEEN RETURNED TO BUCKINGHAM
RETTP TTEETRTR   EE PEAIGPIDAA
PALACE
AANAAT

"But," I objected, "'A partridge in a pear tree,' only has twenty-one letters. What would the coders have done if what they wanted to encrypt had used one of the last five letters of the alphabet."

"I am not sure, but this was not a problem with the message being transmitted and I have in any case provided my own solution to the same problem you stated as you can see on this table."

He went on. "The same code failed to give me a meaning for the second message for the very simple reason that it was marked as having been drafted at 2.23. But using the coding I have outlined for the second verse of *On the First Day of Christmas*, based on Two Turtle Doves gave me:

A	T
B	W
C	O
D	T
E	U
F	R
G	T
H	L
I	E
J	D

K	O
L	V
M	E
N	S
O	A
P	N
Q	D
R	A
S	P
T	A
U	R
V	T
W	R
X	I
Y	D
Z	G

QUEEN GOING TO SANDRINGHAM ON
DRUUS TAEST AA PTSTAESTLTE AS
BOXING DAY
WAIEST TTD

And

BY TRAIN FROM ST PANCRAS AT TEN AM
WD AATES RAAE PA NTSOATP TA AUS TE

"So you were able to decrypt their messages?"

"Indeed so. The other two messages were timed at
3.12 and 3.43 so using as their code the text "Three French
hens, two turtle doves, and a partridge in a pear tree," give:

LEAVING BUCKINGHAM PALACE AT TEN AM

And

TRAFALGAR SQUARE CHARING CROSS
ROAD AND EUSTON ROAD

As usual with Holmes, once the code had been
explained to me, I wondered how I had failed to spot the
solution myself.

"So what was the trap you laid?"

"I used the excellent Hopkins to send them two
messages using their code."

"And they were?"

"Using 'Seven Swans a-swimming' as the basis for
the code for the first message, I wrote giving a time of 7.20.

RETURNING TO LONDON TWO PM THIRTY
DEC EUSTON RD GOWER ST BLOOMSBURY
ST ST MARTINS LANE

"But how did you know on that route the precise
point where the attack on the Queens coach would take
place?"

"The second message I drafted was timed at 8.39
meant that I had to used 'Eight maids a-milking' as the
code. The message I sent was:

ROADWORKS AT JUNCTION OF NEW
OXFORD ST AND BLOOMSBURY ST

I thought the Fenians were bound to see the place
where the roadworks were being carried out as the place to

launch an assault, as the Queen's carriage would have to come to come to a halt there. So I arranged for Lestrade and his men to be at the Rose pub at the junction of New Oxford Street and Bloomsbury so that they could recognise O'Flaherty and his men."

"But how did you arrange for the roadworks to take place?"

"I arranged for some of the Baker Street Irregulars to abstract some traffic barriers and signs indicating roadworks. That signs for roadworks do not mean that any actual road repair work is going on will not surprise anyone used to the ways of London."

"My wound meant that I missed most of the ambush. What happened?"

"A street battle broke out and Lestrade and his men showed great bravery and, though unarmed, they apprehended all the members of the gang."

"Was anyone hurt?"

"As well as your wound, a stray shot from one of the criminals, with whom the brave Hopkins was wrestling, killed one Pierce who works as an attendant of the Prince of Wales. I can only assume that the leak of information about the Queen's movements came from Pierce."

"So a plot to assassinate our Queen has been foiled, the would-be perpetrators of the assassination capture, and the source of it killed."

A rare look of pride stole across my colleague's face.

"Better than that! The fact that the police were on the look-out for O'Flaherty's gang meant that they could attribute the disturbance to their burgling activities and not divulge the breach in royal security. And Lestrade can claim all the credit although the role of Hopkins, who gave me the clue to cracking the code, and who showed great bravery when wrestling with an armed man, also deserves much credit. He will rise within the ranks."

"But surely the full truth will come out."

"You may read about yesterday's events slightly differently in the press."

I must have looked slightly taken aback, and my friend started to explain.

"Here is what *The Times* had to say about yesterday's events.

OFF DUTY POLICE OFFICERS ARREST GUN-WIELDING GANG

The afternoon of the 30th of December saw a most desperate battle between a group of police officers and gang of shop-breakers. A group of officers had met for post-Christmas drinks at the Rose pub at the junction of New Oxford Street and Bloomsbury Street.

The most senior of the policemen, one Inspector Lestrade, spotted idling on the roadway, a man who already known to the police, one Declan O'Flaherty. O'Flaherty is a member of a criminal gang which specialises in shop-breaking.

Lestrade and his officers determined to apprehend O'Flaherty. Although O'Flaherty had appeared to be on his own, there were in fact other gang members in the area, and they fought to prevent the arrest.

A gun was discharged, and one passer-by, a groom in the royal household was killed, and another member of the public was wounded in the leg. Although unarmed, the officers succeeded in overcoming the gang who are all under arrest.

As the gang were armed and were known as burglars, a charge of attempted armed robbery will be brought against them. If found guilty of this charge, the penalty will be severe.

Lestrade's Commanding Officer, whom state security precludes us from naming, commented, "This action is typical of the tenacity of Lestrade and his men. Even armed desperados should be aware that they stand no chance against such determination and courage. I will be recommending the whole squad for gallantry medals."

"I think," said Holmes, "that the public will hear no more about it, but it will be hard for Lestrade's commanding officer not to restore Lestrade to his previous rank."

At that moment a man in a surgical gown came in.

"You had a lucky escape and a lucky break, Doctor," said a man whom I recognised as Stamford who had previously been my wound-dresser at Barts and the man who had introduced me to Sherlock Holmes.

"I had no idea you had risen to become a surgeon, Stamford" said I.

"And I had no idea you would be my patient, Dr Watson," replied he. "I was able to minimise damage from your leg-wound. And while you were under anaesthetic I was able to take a look at your shoulder wound as well. I have done a better job than the surgeon who had to look at it on the battlefield, and I took out some fragments of lead as well as cutting away some scar tissue. It should give you minimal trouble from now on. Indeed, though you will feel pain from your leg, you should barely notice any discomfort from your shoulder."

This case came between *A Study in Scarlet* and *The Sign of Four* and this explains why the first of these mentions a shoulder wound and the latter a wound in the leg. Having read the foregoing, my reader will understand why a veil was drawn over how my wound apparently shifted from shoulder to my leg, and will now also see how Hopkins came to rise from the rank of Constable.

The Book-Thief and the Blitz

I have already disclosed to my reader how in 1940, a few months after the outbreak of what is now known as the Second World War, I moved with my friend Sherlock Holmes to Fenny Stratford in Buckinghamshire. It was only right at the end of that conflict, which surpassed in the number of fallen even the Great War of 1914-1918, that I learned of my friend's role in the breaking of German codes at the nearby house in Bletchley Park.

The few callers at our cottage in Fenny Stratford were generally representatives of the Government seeking my aged friend's help in matters considered too complex for lesser minds and it was on the 10th of November 1940 that we had another caller of this type.

"I am Air Chief Marshall Hugh Dowding," said our tall, slim – rigourous rationing of foodstuffs meant that most of us were very slim at this time – and moustached visitor as he stood before us in his air-force uniform. "I am in charge of the RAF's Fighter Command and so am responsible for the air-defence of this country."

"I am always eager to be at my country's service," said my friend without preamble, leaning forward in his chair.

"The Germans have bombed London nightly for weeks. This is an assault on a civilian population without parallel in the history of warfare. Yet London and Londoners would seem to be able to take it. We think the Germans have started to realise this and we are therefore anticipating a change in enemy strategy."

"Pray continue."

"What I am about to you is a matter of the utmost secrecy. Our intercepts of Luftwaffe wireless traffic have revealed that the Germans are planning something new. They are talking about something called Moonlight Sonata...."

"Mondscheinsonate?" my friend interjected.

"That is what I understand the original German is although it is not a language I speak. But what the moonlight in the name of the Operation may be referring to, is that next week there will be an extremely bright moon and the weather forecast is for clear nights. If they are indeed going to try something different by moonlight, then that may be what they have in mind."

"Although the name given to the operation and the moonlit nights next week may be a coincidence."

"That is so."

"And is that all the information that you have?"

"The Germans dispatches we have intercepted makes references to terms that are obviously code words for something. But we do not know for what."

He handed my friend a piece of paper and Holmes read out.

"'Einheitspreis,' 'Regenschirm,' 'Korn.' These words mean 'standard price' or maybe 'unit price,' 'umbrella,' and 'corn' in English."

"That is what I am given to understand."

"So, you need me to work out what these terms mean."

"That would be the first part of the commission."

"And the second?"

"I cannot impress on you highly enough the importance of the Germans not knowing that we are intercepting their messages. They are referring to their targets by codes and then sending messages in an additional code. Once you have identified the targets, we would like you to travel to them and suggest how they might be defended without the Germans realising that their information has been compromised."

"So you are asking me to do two things that are in fact opposites."

Dowding sat in thought for a few seconds.

"We want to do the maximum we can do defend our cities without the Germans realising we are aware of their plans," he came out with at last. "I feel achieving two opposite objectives is something that can be achieved only by someone endowed with special powers such as you."

"Very well. How do you defend towns at present?"

"The best defence of our country is the fighter. If we are strong in fighters, we should probably never be attacked in force. If we are moderately strong, we shall probably be attacked, and the attacks will gradually be bought to a standstill. If we are weak in fighter strength, the attacks will not be bought to a standstill, and the productive capacity of the country will be virtually destroyed. I would say we are moderately strong in fighters at present, and they can be deployed anywhere at short notice. We can also move heavy guns to defend a position though that takes longer."

"You make yourself very clear."

"The Prime Minister has been most insistent that no measures be taken that jeopardise our access to German data traffic so where a measure might lead the Germans to realise that their information security has been breached, it must not be taken. I may therefore make the argument that we move some guns from one place to another but our scope for action beyond that is limited."

Dowding was soon on his way and Holmes lit his pipe from the dottles of his previous day's supply of tobacco.

"I must," he said drily, "focus on the non-contradictory part of this commission before turning to one which requires me to square the circle of doing two opposite things." He stared down at the three words, repeating "'Einheitspreis,' 'Regenschirm,' 'Korn,' 'Standard price,' 'Umbrella,' 'Corn,'" over and over again.

"These codes must say something to the Germans so that it is obvious what places they are referring to, assuming it is places they are thinking of. And yet they must also be deemed by them to be impenetrable to any outsider," he mused drawing on his pipe.

"Would it be worth thinking about what the target might be?" I asked. "Three railway junctions – Bletchley, Crewe, and Clapham – or three ports – Liverpool, Belfast, and Bristol – or three oil refineries – although I confess I do not know the names of any."

"That is a possible approach," said Holmes cautiously, "but you have hardly narrowed the field. And I imagine, although I do not know, that the three targets would be close to each other."

"Plymouth, Poole, and Portsmouth," I hazarded but got no response.

I decided to leave Holmes to his musings and took up the *Times* newspaper which in this time of stringency appeared in a single sheet folded into two.

The previous day had seen the death of the man who had been Prime Minister until but six months earlier, Neville Chamberlain. It has been said one should never speak ill of the dead and the obituary in *The Times* described Chamberlain as a man of peace without suggesting that it was the failure of his quest for peace which had left this country in its present position of standing alone against an enemy that now occupied almost the whole of Western Europe.

As the writer put it, "Chamberlain was a first-rate mayor of Birmingham with many local successes to his credit. Whether this was sufficient preparation for dealing with a murderous dictator or whether anyone else might have done any better, is not a matter to speculate on today. I nevertheless feel pride at the efforts he made for peace even though in his winged collar and bow-tie, and with his umbrella tucked under his arm, he did rather look like a senior bank-clerk on the way to an assignation with an ogre."

"There's an article here," I said, "which has a major city and an umbrella in the same paragraph."

If an eighty-six-year-old man can spring, Holmes sprang. He seized the newspaper from my hands and read the article through.

"Well," he said eventually, "Birmingham makes sense as a target although with a climate as wet as this country has, many cities may be associated with an umbrella."

"If," I countered, "Birmingham is umbrella, would not the other places be in the same area as you suggested. Could Corn, be Coventry?"

"Corn but not Coventry is spelt with a K in German," countered Holmes although he sounded slightly defensive when he said it. "And if we are looking for an association with corn rather than a similarity of the sound of a word, Brighton, Cambridge, and Norwich have corn exchanges while Coventry does not. And none of this helps us with 'Standard price.'"

"Have you any guesses of your own?"

"I never guess. It is a shocking habit – destructive to the logical faculty."

"So, does your logical faculty give you any ideas?" I retorted, slightly nettled at my friend's dismissal of what I regarded as, at worst, well-intentioned suggestions. "The fate of something or three things key to the war effort is at stake," I added.

Holmes sat back in his seat and said almost to himself. "It must be three things of a kind. And probably three things that are close together. But…" the voice fizzled out and Holmes sat in armchair, his legs drawn up against his chest.

"Let us suggest to Dowding that Umbrella is Birmingham, and that Corn is Coventry and tell him that we are looking to identify the third," he said at last. "It is possible that something else might occur to me though we have no idea of what 'Standard price' is. I will suggest we go to one of these cities to reconnoitre."

So it was that three days later a car, a rarity on the roads of our village at that time, drew up to take us northeast. Coventry was to be our first destination. There was a glass panel between passengers and the driver, so Holmes and I were able to talk freely. "There are munitions factories in Coventry, Watson, so it is an obvious and legitimate target for enemy bombers. Our first appointment there is with the mayor of Coventry. Arthur Grindlay, is a factory owner, and head of the Coventry auxiliary fire service to boot."

"It sounds like Dowding is getting us access to the right person."

The journey is no more than fifty miles but was destined to be a long one as we got a puncture. "Always a problem with the poor-quality rubber we use these days," grumbled Gibb, our driver, as he made an efficient job of changing the tyre. But the night had already fallen by the time we resumed our journey, and we drove in complete darkness in the blackout. It was when we were about five miles from the city that we heard an ominous drone overhead.

"Jerry bombers!" exclaimed Gibb and pulled in at the side of the road. "We will have to stay put here until they are gone."

In the presence of my friend Sherlock Holmes, I have always felt that possibilities were unlimited. But now under the deafening roar of hundreds of bombers, I felt as powerless as when, severely wounded by a Jezail bullet, my orderly was constrained to throw me across the back of a packhorse during the Battle of Maiwand sixty years earlier. We could occasionally hear the pounding of anti-aircraft guns as they sought to bring down the planes, but the raid went on and on.

"I'm used to how they do this from London," said Gibb. "They send over pathfinders to mark a target area. And then the heavy bombers come in with high explosive bombs to smash the roads and buildings inside the target area. They also knock out the water-mains which makes it harder to fight the fires. The ground guns pound away and bring down a few of the Jerry 'planes, but enough bombers always get through."

It was not long before the night sky had turned to blood and, even through the closed car windows, the smell of burning was overpowering. At each report of a landing bomb, I thought the ground around us might heave up its dead, and I was glad beyond relief that we had got no closer than five miles to the city. It was to be half-past-six the next morning before we could drive on, and Gibb stopped by a roadside telephone box to obtain instructions from London.

"I was lucky to get through at all," he said, when he returned to the car. "After a heavy raid the lines are often down. I am to take you to Leicester, where accommodation has been found for you, and you are to stay there to await further orders. All unauthorised travel has been banned across the country, but this is authorised. It's about twenty-five miles to go from here."

We were put up at the Fox Hotel which was open for essential personnel only. As she brought us our meagre breakfast, our waitress said, "On the wireless this morning, all they were saying was that a Midlands industrial town has been hit. But we could see the flames from Coventry from here even though it's twenty miles away, so we knew where it was. Who knows where they will strike next?"

I have seldom seen my friend in a deeper gloom. "We were too late to stop Coventry, and I fear Birmingham is next. And we have made no progress at all on what place is represented by 'Standard price'."

Ae we sat smoking, our waitress came back. "There's a gentleman to see you, Mr Holmes. He is called Mr Richard Broom."

A fresh-faced, smartly dressed man of about thirty came through the door.

"I am afraid, Mr Holmes," said our visitor, "for all wartime secrecy, I saw two men who could only be you and Dr Watson descend from an official car this morning on my way to work. I popped out to see you when I would normally be having my elevenses."

"I am surprised your library is still in operation in these difficult times and I can see you are busy." Our visitor looked stunned, but Holmes added with a look of mild self-satisfaction. "The mark of ink on the tip of each of the two first fingers of your left hand would indicate no other profession that that of a librarian who holds the page to stamp a book out with his left hand while he applies the date-stamp with his right."

"I suppose I should be unsurprised by such wizardry Mr Holmes," replied our visitor and gave us a wan smile. "I do indeed work in one of Leicester's suburban libraries, and it is partly about my work that I wish to speak to you today."

I think my friend had been buoyed by the opportunity to demonstrate his skill at deduction, but I could see that with the grave matters before us that he was surprised by the topic our visitor wanted to raise.

"Librarianship runs in my family and my father, who died of natural causes two weeks ago, was the head librarian at Leicester's central library. My father was a widower, we have or had the same name, and I am his only child. When I was clearing out his house, I found that his attic was full of books."

"Are books not something you would expect to find at a librarian's house?"

"The books had all been stolen from Leicester's libraries. And from libraries further afield."

"So your father was a book thief. And he is now, forgive the reference, no more. Surely at this grave juncture – and I am breaching no confidence when I tell you that only a grave matter can have brought me to Leicester – you cannot expect me to take an interest in an instance of stolen library books."

"The books are all about one subject. That makes the matter doubly mysterious."

"And what is that subject?"

"The history of the city of Leicester."

I cannot imagine a subject which normally have been less likely to interest my friend than the history of an English provincial town. And yet it was a mark of these strange times that now no other subject would have piqued his interest so much as we searched for a solution to a code word which may have had its origins in some overlooked reference to a Midland town.

"The history of the city of Leicester?"

"Yes."

"Had it not been noted that libraries were missing books from their sections on the history of the city."

"I have investigated that point and I think my father was subtle about his theft. He would take books from their dust-jacket and then put the jacket onto a book on another topic and then move that book to the section dedicated to the history of Leicester. That meant that the empty space on the shelf would not be noticeable."

"But surely someone would have noticed that books with a cover referring to the history of Leicester were about a completely different topic."

"Books about Leicester are not of the type to attract many readers and I am not aware that anyone ever reported that any books were missing."

"And did he select the volumes the volumes he stole?"

"He seems to have tried to clear out each library's selection of books on Leicester. In several instances he had the multiple copies of the same book."

"And you want me to investigate the theft of library books at this time when the world is in a crisis unprecedented in its magnitude."

"I cannot help wondering if my father was a German spy," replied Broom, echoing my own thoughts. "Why would a man gather to himself all the books he could lay his hands on about Leicester? And all the thefts had happened in the last two or three years given the dates stamped in the books, the books' condition, and their publication date. Could my father have been looking for something that would be of interest to the Germans?"

101

"Had he ever expressed any pro-German opinions or is your family of German origin?"

"Not that I ever heard about. But I do remember when the Germans introduced what they called blood-purity laws, he commented that at least he had records of where he came from going back several generations. 'We actually might do quite well in a Nazi takeover,' is what he said as I recall although I thought he was joking. I gave the matter no further attention at the time."

"Were there signs he had read the books?"

"He had. A few were in the main part of the house rather than in the attic and he had even cut pages out of some of them. Mostly maps of Leicester."

"What can you tell me about the habits of your father?"

"He had run the city's main library for several years and was an employee of long-standing whom everyone liked and completely trusted. That was why he must have found it easy to take books."

"Was anything else unusual found at his house?"

"Nothing beyond the books about Leicester and the excisions from them I referred to."

"Have you involved the police?"

"I had considered it, but I judged they would have other priorities. I was inclined to let the matter drop until I saw two men answering the description of Mr Sherlock Holmes and Dr John Watson on my way to work this morning. It would seem perverse not to raise this matter with two luminaries such as yourselves in the city."

This time it was Holmes who gave a slightly wan smile.

"Dr Watson has quoted me as saying that a case is always welcome so I will give the matter some thought."

He drew on a cigarette before adding. "Whatever your father was looking for, it must lie in the history of Leicester. I confess this is not a subject I know much about. Perhaps you could give me a brief account of the main events in the city's past."

"My father was an enthusiastic local historian, so he told me about it. Leicester shares a history of conflict common to many older English cities. Its last two syllables mean that the Romans had an encampment here. It was the powerbase of Simon de Montfort, who was Earl of Leicester in the thirteenth century. He founded the English Parliament, and he violently expelled the Jews from here as well as expropriating their property elsewhere in the country. King Richard III spent the night before the Battle of Bosworth in 1484 here before he was defeated by Henry VII in the battle which meant the end of the Wars of the Roses, the end of the House of Plantagenet, and the start of the Tudor dynasty on the throne. It was the birthplace of Lady Jane Grey who tried to usurp Queen Mary and was subsequently beheaded. And in the English Civil War, Leicester was a Roundhead stronghold and was sacked by the Royalists."

"Most colourful. And what is Leicester best known for today?"

Broom paused.

"Even as a proud citizen of Leicester, I struggle to think of many things that make it outstanding compared to other English cities other than the matters I have previously referred to. Our coat of arms bears the de Montfort Fox on a red background. It may be this red background that gives the local Leicester cheese its name Red Leicester even though the cheese is in fact orange in colour and the colour comes from carrot juice."

"And what about its major businesses?"

"Leicester has been linked to the main railway network for the last hundred years and has a wide range of businesses – although clothing and footwear manufacture are the biggest. The League of Nations declared it to be second richest city in Europe after London only four years ago although everything has since been disarranged by the war and most of the manufacture in the city has been turned over to war production."

"So the city is commercially successful?"

"Undoubtedly so."

Holmes lit his pipe and started to smoke. He was not to utter another word and did not respond even after Broom asked whether there were any more questions. After Broom had eventually taken my friend's silence as an indication to leave, Holmes still sat there as if stupefied while I took Broom's contact details.

It was to be another half hour before Holmes finally spoke and I have edited his numerous pauses in my rendition of what he said.

"Are these matters connected? We think there are three targets for bombs. We have speculated – and it is no more than a speculation – that Umbrella is Birmingham, and that Corn is Coventry. And Coventry has now suffered a devastating attack. Assuming no other idea occurs to us about Umbrella, we are left looking for some characteristic that links possible target for bombing to a Standard Price or Einheitspreis. And in Leicester we have this man Broom. Or the deceased Broom senior to be more precise. He is, or was, sufficiently interested in Leicester's history to steal books about it from its libraries and to cut out maps of the city. Are these matters connected? I see no obvious connection between the history of Leicester as it has been told us and anything that might have to do with a Standard or Unit Price."

"Surely the Germans would not waste resources with a spy looking for an obscure reference to provide a code name for the City. If they took an interest in Leicester at all, it would be to know where the gun emplacements were."

"Think of Occam's razor. If we are to assume that the Standard Price mystery and the book theft have two different motivations, we are multiplying our problems, and solving neither."

My reader may imagine that tension was palpable in the air in the city. Air-raid sirens sounded periodically as German planes over-flew us bound I knew not whither while Holmes continued to try to crack the German place name codes.

Three days later, we once again saw the night sky turn to blood.

"Birmingham," I speculated, as I looked west, and wondered how it would all end.

I was unsurprised when the next day Dowding came to see us.

"After the attack on Coventry," he said gloomily, "Hitler's Propaganda Minister, Joseph Goebbels, said that other British cities would be coventried – his own invented verb. And that is what has happened to Birmingham last night. Quite apart from the loss of life, which was considerable, the Birmingham Small Arms plant, the county's sole producer of service rifle barrels and our main aircraft machine-gun manufacturer, was destroyed. I have never seen the Prime Minister so concerned about a loss of production. And beyond the assumption – and it is still an assumption – that the next attack as part of Moonlight Sonata will be somewhere in the English Midlands, we don't know what the target is. There is Derby, Nottingham, Wolverhampton, and Northampton as well as here in Leicester."

Normally when Holmes wanted to reflect, he put himself into a confined space and smoked until the air hung with fumes. Now the three of us went for a subdued walk round Leicester with Holmes on a hunt for filterless cigarettes. "You'd have thought getting hold of cigarettes which require less material to make should be easier in wartime," he complained as we looked for a shop that had not put up its boards. "And a filterless cigarette with nothing between the tobacco and me is just what I need to aid my concentration!"

The few people we saw stood talking in anxious huddles.

"In Coventry," commented Dowding gloomily, "we decided to put the army on the street. Our soldiers have nothing to do at present anyway as we won't be fighting land battles any time soon. When we did it, we said the men were there to help the inhabitants but in fact the real reason why we stationed the troops was to make sure that there was no breakdown of civil order."

Eventually we found that one store – the city's Woolworths – was open. Most of the window was boarded up but in the part where we could see through glass was a chalk board with the Woolworths standard advertising claim saying, "Everything at sixpence – subject to availability."

"Woolworths is one place," I said, in what I confess may have been a slightly ill-judged attempt to lighten the mood, "that has a standard price."

Holmes and Dowding stopped in their tracks and stared at the board.

"Do you have anything more specific in your mind about what Standard Price might mean than what Dr Watson has observed?" Dowding asked Holmes.

"Are you suggesting that every town in the country with a branch of Woolworths is a target?" countered Holmes.

"No," replied Dowding, "but it might be that the German target is Wolverhampton which sounds like Woolworths. As you say, there is a Woolworths in every town in the country. The logic that Standard price is Wolverhampton is no more abstruse a link than Corn for Coventry and Umbrella for Birmingham."

"Air Marshall, how you dispose of your forces is your own matter. It is not my place to recommend acting on a logic of the type you have suggested."

"I have no choice but to act, Mr Holmes. This country's prosecution of this war depends on action." And with that Dowding was off. I felt there was nothing more for Holmes and me to do in Leicester but no trains without a direct military application were yet running. Eventually we were told we would have to wait until the 20th of November for a car to pick us up and take us to Fenny Stratford.

Holmes spent the time we had in a daze. I am not sure how he divided his time between where or what might be represented by Standard Price and what Richard Broom's father might been up to, for he addressed no word to me.

Two hours after the fall of darkness on the 19th of November we heard again heard air-raid sirens and the distant roar of bombers.

"This time it's for real!" cried the waitress who had served us our breakfast on the first day and who had served us with what little food she had available since then. Looking out we saw flames already rising from bombs that must have fallen on the edge of the city. "There are no special shelters built here, but there's a big crypt under the cathedral. Let us go there!"

Mrs Higgins had a torch specially modified for use in the unlit streets of the blackout with a long protruding extension which prevented its beam being visible from above. But, as we hurried up a narrow street called Grey Friars towards the cathedral, we realised this precaution was an irrelevance for the night was aflame as fires licked Leicester's rooftops. Just to our right a bomb had landed leaving a yawning crater in the surface of an area that was kept for parking cars in happier times. Holmes was a few yards ahead of me and I saw him stop and stare down into the chasm that had been created. As I caught up with him, I heard him exclaim, "But of course!"

"We must go to the safety of the cathedral as quickly as we can," I cried. "For all that we cannot find a link between Standard Price and Leicester, this is the city where the attack is."

The air-raid continued all night. We were in the crypt of a church which I subsequently learnt claimed an origin from buildings of Roman times, but nothing felt secure as the vaulted undercroft shuddered under shockwaves from the impact of bombs. I am used to long periods of waiting with Holmes, but we had always been in charge of events. Here, we were at the mercy of where bombs landed and the strength of the tonnes of masonry protecting us above.

It was half-past four the next morning before the all-clear sounded and Mrs Higgins used her torch to guide us through the still dark and rubble-strewn streets to the Fox Hotel. I was soon in my bed, but Holmes shook me awake at first light. "Come Watson, we have a mystery to solve."

"Is there still a mystery to solve?" I asked as I wearily got dressed. "Coventry, Birmingham and Leicester have now all been attacked, even if you have not solved the codenames to your satisfaction."

"As we have heard, Leicester has been attacked in previous centuries and it is a mystery from another conflict that we can now solve to my satisfaction."

By now we were approaching Grey Friars, but we were not destined to get any further for two uniformed Air-Raid Precaution or ARP wardens were barring entry to it. "The street's not safe," they said in unison, "and you can't go up it. There are more UBs down there than you can wave a stick at."

If my reader is wondering, as I was, what the term UB meant, we got an almost immediate answer as we heard the report of two previously unexploded bombs detonating and a loud crash as who knew how many tonnes of masonry fell. A huge pall of dust rose into the grey sky. "I shouldn't think Grey Friars will be cleared till the end of the war whenever that is," added one of the wardens for good measure.

We returned to the Fox to wait in case the car which had been scheduled to pick us up actually made it.

"I fear, good Watson, if you wish to make an account of these matters you may have to have recourse to one of your backstories," said Holmes sucking eagerly at one of the filterless cigarettes he had bought at Woolworths.

"My backstories?"

"Yes, they generally appear, I suspect, when the resolution of the investigation is not satisfactory such as when the malefactor is not apprehended, or when the story is not of the length required by your publisher. I have always disliked them because they take the focus away from me and I am the main reason why your readers read your work."

"Really, Holmes, this is hardly a time for you to preen. For what it is worth, I think it unlikely that an account of what we have seen will see the light of day in our lifetime. Subject to what you may now say, I do not think we have an outcome to any of the matters on which we have been engaged. We may or may not have resolved what the Germans' three targets were, but we can speculate on this only because attacks have been carried out on three major cities with devastating results. Do you have a solution on the theft of the books?"

"Yes, though not one that we can do anything with as I can see no benefit in doing anything with it."

"Are you able to divulge it to me?"

"I will do so on condition that you do not do anything with it either."

I nodded.

"I could see no way the theft of the books could have anything to do with working for the Germans as why would they want a code name for a place that was derived from something that was an obviously obscure piece of history. Yet there were indications in the behaviour of the librarian that he had uncovered some major secret. He was jeopardising his career to abstract books, he was using great cunning to conceal their absence, and he was taking multiple copies of the same book."

I nodded again.

"The latter piece of behaviour implies that he feared that someone else might discover the secret."

"That makes sense."

"As we were going up Grey Friars street last night, the air was illuminated by fires from the bombs, and a bomb had created a huge crater in the street. Lying in the crater, I could see a skeleton."

"I would have thought that dead bodies in the street were not in short supply last night."

"This was a skeleton, not a freshly killed body. And it had a curved spine."

It took a moment for what Holmes was saying to sink in, and I had to dredge up memories of being forced to study Shakespeare at school.

"Are you saying you saw the skeleton of Richard III who was killed at the Battle of Bosworth?"

"There cannot be many skeletons with a curved spine. And that is not the most important part of what I have discovered. It is the coincidence of the name."

"The name? You mean Richard III and Broom's first name Richard? Richard is hardly an unusual name."

"No, it is the coincidence of the Plantagenet house name of Richard III which means the yellow-flowering plant, broom. It was another Richard, Richard of York, and Richard III's father who first used Plantagenet or Broom as the name for his family."

"Are you suggesting that the Plantagenet claimant to the British throne is – "

"Mr Richard Broom to see you again, Mr Holmes," came the announcement from Mrs Higgins.

"Ah, good morning Mr Broom," said Holmes blandly.

"I was passing and saw there is a car outside the hotel. I assume it is to pick you up."

"The habit of deduction is obviously catching."

"I was wondering if you had the chance to look into the little problem I presented to you a few days ago, Mr Holmes. My suburban library is closed today following last night's bombing and I am afraid the main library has been hit."

"I fear that I have been unable to dedicate any time to your mystery."

"It is unpleasant to relate, but my father's house also took a direct hit last night, and so all the evidence of his theft has disappeared. It would appear best to let the matter drop."

"I am sure that is a wise decision, and I would seek to honour your father's memory as a lifelong servant of Leicester rather than waste energy at this difficult time to investigate what he was up to with his book thefts."

"I think you are right, Mr Holmes. Thank you for giving me your time."

In the car on the way back to Fenny Stratford, the glass panel between us and the driver safely closed, I taxed Holmes with what had happened.

"You had a claimant to the throne of England before you and you did nothing?"

"I suspect I would have done the same whether there was a war on or not. There is no point scratching open wounds that are nearly five-hundred years old."

"And was Broom really the last Plantagenet?"

"Richard III's only legitimate offspring died in childhood. Any claim to the English throne Broom would have had, would have been through one of Richard III's numerous siblings. Broom senior would have foreseen he would have rivals to the throne which may explain why he stole books from so many different places to restrict the chances of someone else finding out about it."

"But did he need the body of Richard III to establish his claim?"

"The secret of Richard III's last resting place would have caused a great stir. To have it discovered by someone claiming descent from a Plantagenet would have added to the story's value. Even if he did not claim the throne, being the only person to know where Richard III was buried would have enabled him to make money out of the body's discovery. I do not want to speculate what might happen if the Germans defeat us, but one thing they will want is a new head of state. The recently abdicated Edward VIII may make a more obvious candidate for that role than a distant descendent of a family that last provided a monarch four and a half centuries ago, but Broom senior may have had his own ideas on the matter."

"So what will happen now?"

"In the matter you gave the title, *The Musgrave Ritual*, you described how I found the crown of Charles I. To have a role in the discovery of the body of Richard III would give me huge professional satisfaction but I can think of no time worse suited to exploring this matter. The body may be discovered in the clean-up after the bomb-damage if it was not damaged beyond recognition by last night's bombings."

"And the codes?"

"There were three places mentioned and three places, not previously subject to major raids, have been bombed. I can only assume that Coventry was corn, Birmingham was Umbrella and Leicester, rather than Wolverhampton, was Standard Price even though I see no link between Standard Price and Leicester. All the links between the codes and the bombed towns seem tenuous, and though we can guess –

and I use the term advisedly – why the Germans called Coventry Korn and Birmingham Umbrella, why the Germans chose to call Leicester Standard Price may well become lost in the fog of war."

I sat back in my seat. We were approaching one o'clock and I wondered how the attack on Leicester was being covered on the wireless. I opened the glass panel to the driver, who happened once more, to be Gibb, and he tuned in to the news.

"Last night saw an attack on an east Midland city," was all that the BBC had to say about the events at Leicester, but the news also mentioned that Dowding was standing down from his role as the man responsible for Britain's air defences. The announcement did not provide any reasons for his dismissal but major attacks on three of Britain's most important industrial towns must have been one.

"So that was why Dowding wanted my help!" exclaimed Holmes. "He must have felt under pressure because bombs were raining down on London night after night and saw Operation Moonlight Sonata as an opportunity to turn things round."

Thus matters I have described are more than usually unsatisfactory.

We may have identified some of the targeted towns from their code names, but they had still been subject to savage bombing. We probably had discovered the lost body of an English king but could not raise the matter with anyone. And we had a solution to what Standard Price referred although as my reader will now discover we were definitely wrong on this too and, as Holmes suggested I might, I append a back story, albeit a brief one.

At the end of the war, Hermann Goering, the man responsible for prosecuting the air-war from the German side, was arrested. Holmes and I were asked to be present in Germany to help with the interrogation of the German Nazi grandees, and we were observers when Goering was giving an account of Luftwaffe strategy in 1940. I set out what he said below.

"When making war, as with all other things in life, it is a question of reward and cost. We felt we had done what we could in London and so we switched our attention to bombing English provincial towns which we thought might be less well-defended. They had not yet been attacked, and they were of importance to Britain's war industry. But bombing them was risky as our planes would have to spend a long time over enemy terrain. We initially chose Coventry, Birmingham, and Wolverhampton for our attacks, but our weather forecaster suggested that there were clouds coming in from the west on the night we planned to bomb Wolverhampton, so instead we chose Leicester which is further east and so would not be obscured by clouds until later in the night."

It is perhaps worth dwelling on the randomness of war.

If the weather forecast had been different, the attack on Wolverhampton would have spared Leicester although who knows for how long. The defence of Wolverhampton might have revealed to the Germans that their traffic was compromised although a robust defence might also have saved Dowding's job especially as it would have shown that he was ahead of the great Sherlock Holmes who had not been able to identify what city was going face an attack. And Holmes and I would not know the final resting place of Richard III which is a secret which will have to be left to future generations to discover.

Note by Henry Durham – historical advisor to
***The Redacted Sherlock Holmes* series**

The code names mentioned above are all genuine and the reason for bestowing the names of Corn, Umbrella, and Standard Price on Coventry, Birmingham, and Wolverhampton are as stated in Dr Watson's account of events. No name was ever given to Leicester, but the date and nature of the attack on it is also as stated. Richard III's body, first glimpsed by Sherlock Holmes in the November 1940, was eventually disinterred in September 2012 and Richard III's tomb can now be seen in Leicester Cathedral.

The Sussex Factotum

Helen Stoner's stepfather, Dr Grimesby Roylott, struck her so savagely that he left a visible mark on her which she felt compelled to cover up. He then tried to kill her with a poisonous snake. When Beryl Stapleton threatened to betray Jack Stapleton's plot to kill Henry Baskerville, he first beat her, and then tied her to a pillar in their house. Jephro Rocastle threatened to set his dog on his son's governess, Violet Hunter and kept his daughter locked, like Rapunzel, in a tower. And Violet Smith was kidnapped, gagged, and subjected to a forced marriage which, happily, had no legal validity.

If sensationalism were what I craved in my work, I would have made more of these heinous acts against women. Instead, I set before the public the minimum that was needed to give a sense of what had happened and placed at the forefront of my work the logical mental processes of my friend. In this work, by contrast, the shocking acts set down here for the first time now that their perpetrator is no more, cannot be minimised and their intrusion on the investigation that Holmes and I undertook was such that they became an entirely unanticipated centrality to it. I nevertheless have disclosed the minimum I can confine myself to in order to describe these so outré matters and, if my readers might wonder what else I might have said, I would advise them to give their worst imaginings a free rein. My readers will also note the very limited role of my friend Mr Sherlock Holmes in this account of events. So bizarre are the matters I describe that maybe it was not so much that they were beyond his powers, but that they occupied some alternative reality where those powers no longer held sway.

In the 1920s and 1930s I still maintained my medical practice in Queen Square. At this period of my life, Sherlock Holmes had passed almost beyond my ken although he still continued to make occasional use of my house as a meeting place when he had an appointment in London. It was thus not a complete surprise when my receptionist came into my consulting room one morning in April 1932 and said, "A Mr Sherlock Holmes rang and asked to see you, Dr Watson. He is waiting for you at the Langham Hotel."

As my readers will be aware, I have never found my practice particularly engaging. Thus, the choice between listening to my patients' seemingly intractable complaints and meeting my friend, Sherlock Holmes, at an establishment which featured both in *A Scandal in Bohemia* and in *Lady Frances Carfax,* was always going to be a simple one. It was the work of a moment to give my staff the afternoon off and to refer my waiting patients to the practice next door where, I assured them, my neighbour would be delighted to take their custom. A few minutes, and I was striding round the corner to Russell Square Station, and a few minutes more saw me turning into Langham Place with its famous hotel at the corner. Holmes, lean as ever, was waiting for me in one of the hotel's grandiose ground-floor smoking rooms.

"My dear fellow," said I, "what a pleasure that you are here."

Holmes was not effusive, but he was, I think, pleased to see me.

"We will," he said, "shortly be joined by my brother, Mycroft, who has advised me that he has a matter to put to us," – how my heart leapt at the use of the word "us"! – "that, he says, is too delicate for communication in writing."

A few minutes after this saw Mycroft, as rotund as he had been in the 1890s, enter. He sat for several minutes, as though not sure how to open his disquisition.

"And yet," he said at last, looking around him, "what is it that makes me vacillate? The matter is in the public domain. There have even been questions asked about it in the House of Commons. Why do I hesitate about bringing it to your attention?"

"Why indeed?" murmured his brother.

"Very well. Then both of you should be aware that even in my advanced years I am still in the occasional employ of this country's government which confides in me when there is no one else obvious to confide in. Thus, while it is no longer true to say that I *am* the British Government, I remain its advisor of last resort."

"Pray continue."

"As you will both know, this country has set up the world's first wireless broadcasting company and it has been in operation since 1923. The British Broadcasting

Corporation is in the process of moving into new headquarters which are within a minute's walk from here. It is considered appropriate for the building's façade to be adorned with statues and a man called Eric Gill has been commissioned to provide one of these which will go above the main entrance. It is to feature the subject of Prospero and Ariel."

"From Shakespeare's *The Tempest?*" I offered, dredging up unwelcome memories of studying the bard at school.

"Quite so, dear doctor," replied Mycroft, looking slightly distrait. "Prospero is a sorcerer and Ariel is a spirit in his service. Prospero is normally portrayed as a man of mature years and Ariel as a child."

"Why should a broadcaster's headquarters be adorned by a statue of Prospero and Ariel?" asked Holmes.

"I do not know," replied Mycroft shortly.

"Could it be a word play on the use of an ariel or antenna to get reception of broadcast signals?" I hazarded.

"Very possibly so," replied Mycroft, for once looking very much not like someone who specialism was omniscience. "I confess that I had not given the matter any thought."

"Then why have you brought us here?" asked Holmes.

"The portrayal of Ariel has caused something of a furore amongst those who have been given a sight of it."

"How so?"

For a man normally so little given to uncertainty, Mycroft seemed the victim of a paroxysm of doubt. He again looked around him.

In the end he came out with, "It has been suggested that the portrayal of the young Ariel has a disproportionate development in one particular respect. We have commissioned an expert in Shakespeare who has opined that Ariel should be portrayed as a boy of about thirteen." Mycroft, his grey eyes normally so masterful, now seemed to cast his gaze in all directions and nowhere at once. He took a huge pinch of snuff and in the end came out with. "It is perhaps appropriate that the young boy portrayed should be called Ariel as is it in the part of the body most like an ariel that the portrayal is thought by some to be disproportionate for a boy of thirteen."

Once Mycroft had finally found a formulation of his petition that he was comfortable to use to vouchsafe it, he suddenly became once more all self-assurance, and continued. "On behalf of the government, I have decided I need to take medical advice to establish whether this perception is justified."

"So why do you need to see me on this matter? Surely if this…" asked Holmes.

"Dr Watson," said Mycroft, cutting across his brother and turning to address me, "as a physician, you are the person from whom I have decided to seek this medical advice. No one will think to question any judgment that is reached by a figure as reliable and well-known as you. Let us go to the entrance of Broadcasting House now and you can pass the qualified opinion of a medical man."

It was only a few minutes before we stood beneath a large tarpaulin.

"When questions were first raised," said Mycroft, "I was able to prevail on the authorities to have the statue covered up. But now it will be uncovered for your perusal." At a signal from Mycroft to the doorman, the statue was freed from its drapes.

As soon as it became visible, it was obvious to me that the matter was as Mycroft had stated.

I expressed my opinion to him, and he said, "It is good to have clarity on this point. Gill has refused point blank to modify the statue, but we have someone else able to make the necessary adjustments now that the matter has received the subject of a trusted medical opinion. I shall make sure that all the pictures of it in its current state are destroyed."

A couple of minutes more and we were walking back towards the Langham Hotel, and behind me I could already hear the grating of chisels on stone as the work on making the necessary modifications to the offending part of the statue got underway.

"So good brother," interjected Sherlock Holmes, a note of impatience in his voice, as we arrived back in Langham Place, "the question you have raised is now closed and, as a medical matter, I was never going to be engaged for it. Why have you caused me to come all the way up here from my Sussex fastness when you could have confined your consultation to Dr Watson?"

"Let us return to the smoking-room," replied Mycroft, continuing to look evasive.

When we had we sat down, Mycroft continued. "Mr Gill is something of an *enfant terrible*. His earliest well-known work is the Stations of the Cross at Westminster Cathedral. These are fourteen limestone reliefs of the Passion and Gill got the commission in 1913 when he had very little experience working as a sculptor. His call-up for war-service up was delayed in order to allow him to complete it. Soon after the war he was commissioned to create a war memorial at the University of Leeds and on it he included a relief which featured Christ casting the money-lenders out of the temple. This choice of subject seemed to have no relevance whatever to a war-memorial and caused huge offence in Leeds which is a thriving commercial centre."

"Pray continue."

"And yet in spite of that controversy, and other like the one we have seen today, Gill seems able to get commissions almost at will. He paints, he sculpts, and he designs buildings and typefaces. You may not know his works in forms that most people think of as art, but as well as his pictures and his sculptures, his type-faces are used everywhere including on every map displayed or used by the London Underground and are to be found on the fascia of every branch of the stationer WH Smith including their outlet in Paris. A recent edition of the complete works of the most widely read German poet, Goethe, used a typeface by him. I have worn out shoe-leather and travelled by numerous types of conveyance to many different places to survey his works. In the end I have found it easier" – a weary look came over Mycroft's face as he said this, and he paused to mop his brow – "to find places where his work is not represented."

"So something of an all-rounder?" I commented.

Mycroft adopted a most injured expression at my remark and looked down at his own portly figure.

"It is a cricketing term," I hastened to add as Mycroft opened his mouth to object to the word I had used. "Just as Gill seems to produce work in every medium, so an all-rounder at cricket can both bat and bowl effectively. James Langridge of Susse…"

"Mr Gill," interjected Mycroft, the shadow leaving his face as the realised the term all-rounder did not refer to him, "is also originally of Sussex, but I think I would prefer to regard his eclecticism and prolixity as making him a sort of artistic factotum, a mixture of an artist and a craftsman, rather than the somewhat ambiguous term you have chosen to use."

"So what is it that you want me to do, Mycroft?" interjected Holmes.

"There is concern at the highest level as to how Gill gets such frequent and such diverse commissions which he uses to produce such controversial works. I would like you to explore how this is happening. Does Gill have some sort of hold over the committees of worthies who dispense these commissions? Is he passing bribes for all that such worthies generally have well-upholstered wallets? Or is he blackmailing them for all that the people who are generally selected for leading blameless private lives rather than for having any noteworthy talents?"

"May it not simply be that Gill has found the knack of working to a time and at a price that makes his work attractive to these committees?"

"That may of course be so," said Mycroft thoughtfully. "No scandal has emerged to date either about Gill or the people who have given him the commissions. Indeed, given the longevity of some of those worthies, it is unsurprising to note that some of them like Cardinal Bourne at Westminster Cathedral are still in post."

"And may not some organizations welcome the controversy Gill's pictures engender as they bring attention to the buildings where they are sited and so to the organizations housed in them?"

"All of what you say is possible, dear brother. It would certainly be preferable if the reasons you state were the cause of the facility with which he obtains commissions as opposed to anything …untoward being afoot."

"What can you tell me about Gill?"

"He was born in 1880, the son of an Anglican clergyman who produced a family of twelve children who survived into adulthood. Over his life he seems to have chased up every…." – Mycroft broke off to consider what word to use next – "modish cause that has come to the fore in the country. So, he associated with the socialist Fabians before converting to Roman Catholicism shortly before the

First World War even though several of his siblings had followed their father into the Anglican Church. When he converted, the rest of his family converted as well, and his wife even went as far as to change her name from Ethel to Mary. Mr Gill is also an avowed and vocal pacifist, and it is as well that no war is seen as likely at this time as he would doubtless rail against it and reduce the number of men willing to serve."

"He seems to have eclectic tastes."

"Indeed so. He was born in Sussex and lived in London for several years before returning to live in Sussex. He has lived with his family and friends in what I can only call a succession of communes, first in Sussex, then in Wales, and finally now in the Chilterns in a settlement called Piggots near High Wycombe. He spends his days dressed in a cassock and a cowl like a monk. Although he is the father of three children, he uses a girdle of chastity as to bind his cassock..."

"A girdle of chastity?" I queried.

"It is a girdle the Virgin Mary used as a token of her immaculate state and which she is supposed to have dropped to the doubting St. Thomas when she ascended to heaven." Mycroft paused to take another large pinch of snuff and it was quite a minute before he continued, "I understand that in almost every respect his household is most irregular by the standards of this decade."

"How so?"

"The family cooks at an open fire, draws water from a well in the garden, and has no motorised transport even though they would have the means to afford all the modern conveniences that have made open fires, wells, and the like obsolete. Their children were educated at home. I understand they spend much of the day kneeling on the floor in worship of the Almighty."

"You are surely not implying that Mr Gill obtains his commissions because of his devotion to prayer?" objected Holmes.

"I confess, dear brother, I would be surprised if that were a conclusion you come to me with after your investigation. If that were indeed so, I would feel obliged to suggest to the Prime Minister that he promotes the value of prayer as a means of boosting this country's fortunes."

I have seldom seen my friend look so nonplussed. He puffed at his pipe for several minutes before venturing another question.

"If Mr Gill lives in a Roman Catholic commune, is it not highly improbable that he has the means to bribe or the inside information to blackmail organizations as large and diverse as the Roman Catholic Church, the University of Leeds, the British Broadcasting Corporation, and WH Smith?"

Mycroft shrugged.

"That, dear brother, is for you to find out. It is you who advocate eliminating the impossible to isolate the however improbable truth. Gill's success in gaining such prestigious commissions in such a diversity of forms is certainly remarkable. I am at your disposal if you wish to consult with me on this matter but the minutiae of any investigation I will leave in your hands." And without another word Mycroft was gone, leaving Holmes and me at our pipes in the smoking room.

"I take it," I said, unable to keep a note of excitement out of my voice, "that our next step will be to break into Gill's commune to find out what is happening."

"Ever the man of action, dear Watson," replied Holmes, a trace of smile upon his features. "It strikes me that a more lawful though less dramatic alternative would be to investigate the decision-makers who have awarded Gill his commissions." He glanced at his watch. "It is still not yet twelve. Let us to Westminster Cathedral and see Francis Bourne. Mycroft has informed us that he remains in post as Cardinal and was in office when Gill got the commission to portray the Stations of the Cross. Obtaining his insights must be the way this investigation must begin."

From Langham Place it was no more than a short Underground ride to Victoria Station and then a short walk to the massive brick edifice which is London's Roman Catholic cathedral. Holmes handed in his visiting card and, as was so often the case, it received immediate recognition. We were told that the Cardinal would be free to see us in half an hour. We spent the time inside the cathedral where Gill's massive Stations – more carvings in stone than statues – were mounted. I am not a religious man and have no particular interest in art, but I was struck by the solemnity and craftsmanship that had gone into them.

Soon we were before the Cardinal, a white-haired man in his sixties.

"You want to ask me why we gave the commission for the Stations of the Cross to Gill even though he had little relevant experience?" he asked in some surprise when Holmes put to him the subject of his enquiry. "But that was nearly twenty years ago. How can it be of interest now?"

"I am not at liberty to disclose that to you other than to say that Gill seems remarkably adept at obtaining commissions."

A twinkle came into the Cardinal's eye.

"In the case of our Stations of the Cross, it was all a matter of chance. The money for the Stations was set aside from other funds, and the church governors were anxious to see it spent. We wanted to have an original work rather than something a church furnishing company might provide. In the end, after much unfruitful and sometimes acrimonious discussion, I said to my fellow governors that I would award the commission to the first Roman Catholic I saw. Gill was in the right place at the right time and demanded a price that was within our means."

"Were his Stations in any way…" Holmes paused as he considered the right word, "controversial?"

"They divided opinion – especially the tenth Station where Gill used his own face as a model for Our Lord being stripped of his clothing. At the time Gill was a recent convert to the faith. Since then, he has been a useful supporter to the church – he has even come out in favour of the church's teaching on birth control which is something not many other prominent Roman Catholics have done. I fear gentlemen there is nothing for you to investigate with

Gill much though I would be thrilled to appear as a character in a work featuring the great Sherlock Holmes."

Not many minutes more saw Holmes and me back on Victoria Street. "I do not know what there is to find in this case," commented Holmes. "Competent workmanship and acceptable prices are a good combination though a disappointing trove for someone who remains the world's only consulting detective. And having a work of art with some controversial features may indeed be what the committees commissioning these works want to attract attention. And while the controversy engendered may put off some commissions, it will serve the purpose of attracting attention to the artist which may in turn bring in more commissions. Nevertheless, let us not be disheartened at the first stage of our investigation."

So it was, that the next few weeks saw the two of us criss-crossing the country and interviewing the worthies from many different organizations who had given Gill his commissions. Each time we heard variants of what the Cardinal had told us. The blandness of the responses we obtained seemed only to motivate Holmes to investigate further but with the same result. It was one evening as we sat over our pipes at my house that Holmes said, "It's no good, Watson. All my instincts tell me there is something amiss and yet I find nothing. I fear we will have to stage the break-in at Piggots which you originally advocated."

"Will we not be putting ourselves hopelessly in the wrong in the eyes of the law?" I asked even though the prospect of an unannounced visit to the quarters of our quarry filled me with the excitement I had not known since my halcyon days in Baker Street.

"I will set myself up at Gill's Chiltern retreat," said Holmes, ignoring my question, I expect because he felt the same surge of excitement as I did, "and will call for you when my investigations identify that an opportunity for ingress presents itself."

It was no more than a couple of weeks before I received a telegram from Holmes asking me to meet him at High Wycombe station at six o'clock the next evening. He greeted me as I stepped from the train.

"I have spent two weeks attached to Gill's commune. It is a strange thing to be in such an establishment, especially one, that as my brother says, eschews all modern conveniences. It is perhaps as well that I presented myself as a penniless friar in a cassock for it is only to a mendicant that such a place might appear normal. They took me in, have treated me hospitably, and I have engaged in debate on a wide range of subjects with Mr Gill."

"You disguised yourself as a friar!" I exclaimed.

Holmes raised his hat to reveal a tonsured head.

"Such are the sacrifices one makes for an investigation, but this will grow back in a few weeks, and I can cover up its absence in the meantime. I have had to dedicate myself to oblations to an extent I have never felt the need to before. My knees are sore with kneeling and another visitor to the Gill household was so wearied by the constant devotions that he fainted. But I have established that the occupants of the Gill house including sundry irregular visitors and hangers-on will decamp on a pilgrimage to Walsingham tomorrow morning so the house will be empty. And that is our opportunity. I have taken a copy of a key so the way for us is clear."

After a night at The Nightingale Inn in High Wycombe, we sallied forth at ten o'clock the next morning. Holmes had had made up the uniforms of commissionaires so that we could approach the house without attracting attention and we were inside in the blink of an eye.

"You go through the shelves, and I will search the desk," he said and away we went.

I had the curious feeling as I did as Holmes had bidden that I was being watched, but I could find no reason for my instinct and in the end dismissed it. We had been methodically going through papers for about half an hour when the front door suddenly opened and seconds later a brisk looking woman in her early fifties in round rimmed glasses strode into the room.

"Friar Cuthbert," exclaimed she, looking my friend up and down. "So, you are really Sherlock Holmes and I assume that this is Dr Watson!"

My friend and I were dumbstruck and in the end it was Mrs Gill who broke the silence.

"I did wonder, Mr Holmes, about Friar Cuthbert's arguments with my husband on whether the existence of God could be proved. It was amusing to hear both my husband and you in your disguise use the argument that if you eliminate the impossible, the truth however improbable must emerge to argue both for and against His existence. I thought at the time that the main point of interest of the debate was that the viewpoint Friar Cuthbert expressed eliminated the argument that he was a *bona fide* friar. And so it has proved."

Again no comment from either Holmes or me.

"I felt somewhat faint at the station," Mrs Gill continued, as though to explain her unexpected presence, "and in the end felt I could not go to Walsingham. I suppose you are here to investigate my husband. I had wondered whether something like this might happen someday. As I still feel a bit giddy, I had better sit down if you wish to talk to me."

She pulled a chair over and sat down and as she did so a golden Labrador dog emerged as if from nowhere in the room and placed itself on the floor behind her legs. It looked furtively out at Holmes and me from this strange vantage point.

"Perhaps you could elaborate, Madame," said my friend who had looked mortified by our discovery, but had recovered something of his composure now that Mrs Gill had said something that there was indeed some secret about Gill that we had as yet been unable to uncover.

"You have said Mr Holmes that little things are infinitely the most important. Yet in your time here, I can only assume, to investigate my husband, you seem to have missed the obvious. Your associate Dr Watson is clearly engaged in examining the bookshelves while you are going through my husband's desk."

"If I may be open with you, madam, we are investigating how your husband is so adept at obtaining such a variety and quantity of commissions."

Mrs Gill's eye's opened wide behind the scholarly lenses of her spectacles betraying what looked to me like surprise.

"Ah, well in that case, the answer is... well, the answer is really the same as if your investigation were about what I thought it would be about. Let us go the living-room next door."

Around a long low table were three sofas and Mrs Gill took her place on one and the dog assumed its same strange station staring out at us from behind her legs. She leant forward and picked up a large book.

"My husband," she said, "is an extraordinary and saintly man. Indeed, when we are at prayer, I often fancy I see a nimbus shadowing his features."

"A nimbus?" queried I, though I had a faint recollection of what it was from my divinity lessons which I had enjoyed even less than the lessons I had had on Shakespeare.

"It is," said Mrs Gill in explanation, "a luminous vapour which wreathes the features of a person of great saintliness. I am not the only one who claims to have seen it adorn my husband's brow."

She paused and looked into the distance.

"Are you suggesting, Madame, that it is your husband's saintliness that is gaining him these commissions?" asked Holmes at last, sounding more uncertain about how to proceed than I had ever heard him.

"Good heavens, no!" exclaimed Mrs Gill. "Of course not. My husband is an astute businessman. His first major achievement was getting the commission for the Stations of the Cross at Westminster Cathedral. I am sure he got it because he could come up with a devotional work at a low price. He had it all down here in his daily journal in which he also kept his accounts. He showed me his financial results here."

She passed over the bulky volume open on one page to my friend and I looked across from my seat next to him. There on fine paper in the small, neat handwriting that one might expect from someone who had made his name in devising fine lettering, was a profit and loss account setting out the value of the commission, and the details of the costs incurred to fulfil it. The work had taken Gill four years and he had claimed only six-hundred and sixty-five pounds (Editorial note: in 2024's money about £65,000 or USD 75,000) for it before all his expenses of materials and assistants. I could see my friend's face fall at yet another iteration of what we had heard at so many places.

I think Holmes was wondering what to say next, for there was a silence. It was at this point that my eyes chanced to look over at the page opposite the summary of income and expense for the Stations. To my complete horror and amazement, I saw a reference to an act of which I could not possibly provide any details here but I would advise my readers to give free rein to their worst imaginings. The counter-party was referred to as Petra. I felt I had no choice to raise the matter even though Holmes had made no reference to it.

"Mrs Gill," I said, "there is a description here of something which I cannot bring myself to repeat. It took place between your husband and someone called Petra."

"Ah, that would be our eldest daughter."

A similar look of horror and astonishment crossed the face of my friend as he read what Gill had written on the page opposite the financial summary of his activities at Westminster Cathedral. But he stayed silent, and Mrs Gill continued.

"My husband," said she in a matter-of fact-tone, "is a holy man and I am unworthy of him in every way. We remain a couple married, if I may say, in every sense of the word. But he has urgings he feels he has no choice but to surrender to. He has surrendered to these urgings with a string of mistresses, women of low repute, domestic servants, and with members of his family."

"Members of his family?" I asked barely able to believe my ears and in my horror speaking ahead of Holmes which is never my custom.

"Well, his sisters and daughters."

Holmes continued to look as though he had seen a ghost, and in the end I felt it fell to me to speak.

"And you have no objection to his activities?"

"I would refer you to my previous remarks about my husband's saintliness. Our Lord Himself had an association with the fallen Mary Magdalene which not everyone might approve of."

"And your husband has diarised these activities and no attempt was made to conceal the recording of them?"

"Dear Eric diarises everything. That is why you have seen the recording of all his diverse activities in one place. In a commune such as ours no one has any secrets from anyone else anyway so there seemed no point concealing the diary. I imagine everyone here is aware of his actions. Indeed, many people have been the subject of them. I did wonder whether anyone might talk as he became better known but no one ever has. As you will recall, I was not so surprised that someone chose to investigate my husband, but this diary is rather like the document which disclosed the location of King Charles I's crown in *The Musgrave Ritual* – not something we took pains to conceal. In a sense, my husband's activities have been hidden in plain sight."

"Do you not see any harm in this?" I asked.

"No one has come to any harm. My daughters and sisters-in-law have made good marriages and have children of their own. As well as our grand-children, we also have a full complement of nephews and nieces, and all either live here or are regular visitors. The only member of the household who seems to have come to any harm," she replied, "seems to be poor Sheba here," she patted the head of the Labrador still cowering behind her legs, "who has never been quite as confident since my husband carried out an experiment on her. You can find out about it in that journal. Maybe Dr Watson," she added brightly, "if you choose to make a record of our discussion, you could refer to the singular incident of the dog, although the experiment I referred to took place in the daytime."

I could provide more detail of what Mrs Gill said but I feel that would titillate rather than inform. In not many minutes after the above exchange, there seemed no more to discuss. Holmes and I headed to High Wycombe station and less than an hour later we arrived at Marylebone Station with Holmes having said not a word. No matter we had ever investigated had brought on him the look of repugnance I saw now on his face.

"It is only a few minutes from here to Baker Street, dear Watson," said he in a tone that sounded half-strangled. "Let us go there to get a reminder of a reality I am comfortable with." Although 221 B was no longer accessible to us, it took only a few puffs of his pipe on the pavement outside before he felt sufficiently soothed to glance at his watch and say, "Let us now to the Diogenes Club. That is where we will find Mycroft at this time."

"So, good Sherlock," said Mycroft after his brother had debriefed him, "you have found nothing untoward in the commissions Gill has fulfilled but much that is unorthodox in his private life. I suppose, as with other matters like this, we have the usual four options."

"There are other matters like this?" asked Holmes, sounding more startled than I have ever heard him.

"I extend to other parties, good brother," replied Mycroft smoothly, "the same secrecy that I extend to you."

"And who is the 'we' in your last comment?"

"I am the British government's advisor of last resort. It will do as I say on a matter such as this."

"So what are the four options?" I asked, startled that there could be so many.

"We could put Gill on trial but the only party who seems to show obvious effects from Gill's activities is the family dog whom a court may consider an unreliable witness."

"What about Gill's sisters and daughters?" I asked.

"They may not even want to appear as witnesses. And of course, Gill himself may state that his diary entries merely reflect his imaginings but not his actual deeds which it would be very hard to disprove if his family refused to testify. His other liaisons are not a matter for legal action."

Another pause and this time a pinch of snuff and Mycroft continued.

"As an alternative, we could take down his works without prosecuting him but, as I observed, when I gave you this commission, taking down everything to do with Gill would be an enormous task given their ubiquity and prominence. And it would give rise to questions about the reasons to which we could not give a satisfactory answer to if all the maps of the London Underground suddenly bore a new type face."

He paused once more before he went on.

"A third option would be to take steps to prevent Gill getting new commissions. But prevailing upon every group of worthies in the country not to give as well-known an artist as Gill commissions can also hardly fail to give rise to awkward questions."

Mycroft's face brightened at this point, and I realised what the fourth option was.

"Or we could do nothing and hope nothing comes out. Gill is in his early fifties and cannot go on for ever. Nothing is yet in the public domain about his proclivities and they date back over several decades. I really think that that is the easiest solution to follow."

"We will do nothing to a man who has committed these depraved acts. And may continue to do so? And, from what Mrs Gill tells, he will have every opportunity to continue to do so as he lives in close quarters with people of several different generations," I pressed.

"If we put him on trial," countered Mycroft, "it will make his acts appear normal to some of the more easily led members of the public. And will give rise to the question of whether his activities should not have been discovered sooner and of who knew about them and when. The judgment of many prominent and well-regarded people will be called into question. And it will also be asked whether those who ought to have known actually approved of them or partook in similar things themselves. The outcome of the further investigations which might follow is hard to predict. And impossible to control."

"So, you will suppress my findings?" said Holmes speaking for the first time in a while.

"Indeed, not dear brother. Suppression of anything is not the way we do things in this country. It is the device of demagogues and dictators. As the people's representatives, we in the government will take the decision on the people's behalf not to take any action arising out of your findings. To suppress something and not to do anything about it are not at all the same thing."

"Although they have the same consequences."

"In this instance, that is so. But suppression normally involves the threat or the use of force. What I will recommend to the Prime Minister is the path of inaction. Knowing when to act and when not to act is one of the faculties which has made this country what it is."

Mycroft paused. He took another large pinch of snuff and for once a look of real feeling came into his masterful grey eyes.

"Eric Gill is a troublemaker. A pacifist, a Roman Catholic, and a Socialist. All these causes are deleterious to this country's best interest. I have no doubt Mrs Gill will tell him about your somewhat clumsy intrusion in the Gill house as soon as he gets home from his pilgrimage. The causes Gill espouses will continue whether he is at liberty or not. It is better that their most eloquent and best-known supporter is someone I can control and who knows I can ruin him in an instant than that they be represented by someone whom I know nothing about. If that means that Gill continues with his other practices, then that is a price that will have to be paid."

"But by his family not by you."

"To govern is to choose and that is the choice I have made. The position of the government's advisor of last resort was never intended to be an easy one."

There was a long pause.

My reader will have noted that the comments in response to what Mycroft said are often not attributed and that is the horror I felt was such that I am not always sure who said them. I saw the horror I felt at what Mycroft was saying reflected on Holmes's face and in the end it Mycroft who spoke next.

"And now, gentlemen, if you will excuse me, dinner is served here at the Diogenes, and I would ask you to make your own way out." He rose and went to the door of the Stranger's Room but then turned round and came back to us. I had no idea what he would say next but all he came out with was, "And good Doctor, I would bid you not to set a word of this matter to paper in Gill's lifetime," before he headed once more to the door and this time went through it.

Even several years after the events I have described and following the recent death of Eric Gill, I still shudder at what Holmes and I discovered. And I note that while the abusers of women that I mentioned at the head of this account of events all suffered a downfall, Gill was at liberty to carry on as he wished.

But while it was notable that in his later years Gill continued to get a stream of commissions from various public organizations, he toned down his public comments about the causes he supported. It may of course be that he came to view his advocacy of pacifism as untenable as the drums of war beat louder and louder the longer the 1930s went on. I also noted a magazine interview in which he commented that he had now adopted many of the conveniences of the twentieth century such as running water and electricity in his house although he attributed his adoption of these to the exigencies of old age.

For my own part I cannot help wondering whether the modifications in his behaviour on the two topics I have noted above were because he knew that the matters I have described were something that the British government was also aware of but was making no attempt to use.

I leave open the question of what impact this knowledge had on the third form of behaviour I have referred to but would point out that Gill continued to live in an isolated commune where he was regarded as a demigod and where people of three different generations were always rubbing shoulders with each other. My own surmise is that the knowledge that the British authorities knew of his activities but had chosen to do nothing about them will only have emboldened him.

Note by Henry Durham – historical advisor to
***The Redacted Sherlock Holmes* series**

Eric Gill (1882 to 1940) was a prolific artist and designer.

He left over seven-hundred sculptures as well as fonts such as Gill Sans, Perpetua, and Joanna Nova which remain in use to this day.

Gill's activities with his household members were not mentioned in the first biography of him by his friend, Robert Speaight, which was published in 1966. It was as only in 1989 that Fiona MacCarthy's biography made revelations that shocked the world.

The debate on what to do with his works continues.

The statue of Prospero and Ariel at Broadcasting House which was the starting point of this account of events was attacked in both 2021 and in 2023 but repaired. It remains in place at the time of writing in 2024.

Dr Watson's private papers were rediscovered in the Public Record Office at Kew in 2015 and the process of editing them has continued ever since. They have provided a new light on many historical events and in the account of events here we have for the first time an explanation of why officers of the British State turned a blind eye to Gill's activities for so long.

The Doctor and the Demon

"Come, Brown," answers the master. "I'm beginning to understand the game of cricket scientifically. What a noble game it is, too!"

"Isn't it? But it's more than a game. It's an institution," said Tom.

"Yes," said Arthur – "the birthright of British boys old and young, as *habeas corpus* and trial by jury are of British men."

> Thomas Hughes, *Tom Brown's School Days*

For the field is full of shades as I near the
shadowy coast,
And a ghostly batsman plays to the bowling of a
ghost,
And I look through my tears on a soundless-
clapping host
As the run-stealers flicker to and fro,
To and fro:-
O my Hornby and my Barlow long ago!

> Francis Thompson, *At Lords*

Cricket is a game that is all things to all men.

The science the schoolmaster mentions in *Tim Brown's School Days*, the recognition by Tom Brown that it represents all that is good with this country, the death-haunted nostalgia of Thompson – all these themes and more are handled in the matters I recount below although my reader is warned that the ending is as troubled as Thompson's achingly sad poem.

The Battle of Maiwand took place in July 1880, yet the first collaboration undertaken by Holmes and me, with a specific date, *The Noble Bachelor*, did not occur until 1887. I have yet to disclose the date that I met my friend Mr Sherlock Holmes, but my reader will know it cannot have been long after the Afghan War battle for I am described at the time of our first encounter as being tanned brown as a nut by the colonial sun. The work that follows bridges some of the time between our adoption of Baker Street as our home and the dated first cases we undertook together.

In those early years in Baker Street, my nerves still shaken to the core by my time in my country's service at the battle I refer to above, my army pension stood at eleven shillings and sixpence a day. Once I had met essentials such as rent and tobacco, this was barely enough to live on, and I had two means of supplementing my income. I engaged in speculations on the turf and on the stock market which sometimes paid off, and sometimes, I fear, did not. And I took on short-term medical engagements where I thought the stress might be bearable for my constitution.

These engagements took a variety of forms.

Sometimes I would attend executions to certify that the condemned had actually died in accordance with the laid down protocols. On other occasions I would attach myself to a medical practice and fill in when there was a temporary need. These engagements were by their nature brief and by no means uninteresting but never threatened to overtax my nerves.

Another short-term engagement of this type arose early in my time at Baker Street during the summer of 1882. A party of Australian cricketers was touring the country and their matches attracted high attendances and full coverage in the national press. A challenge match between the Australians and an eleven of the best English players from across the land was scheduled to take place at London's Kennington Oval starting on Monday the 28th of August. I was contracted to be the physician to the English cricketers. They had gathered at a London hotel from the 23rd of that month to acquaint themselves with each other and to prepare themselves for the fixture, and I had an appointment to meet the captain, Mr Hornby on that evening.

The summer of 1882 represented one of the deepest low points in the mental health of Sherlock Holmes as ennui, his constant danger, made him succumb to his personal demon, the dreaded cocaine. At our first meeting he had said, "I get in the dumps at times, and don't open my mouth for days on end. You must not think I am sulky when I do that. Just let me alone, and I'll soon be right." I gave far more coverage to this aspect of my friend in *The Sign of Four* and that work ended with Holmes injecting yet another dose of cocaine into his veins but this rebellion against what he saw as the drabness of existence had much earlier manifestations.

My reader may imagine that the prospect of attending to a team of cricketers in the prime of their youth and living with a man addicted to the numbing influence of cocaine were difficult things to combine. While I was comfortable ministering to what was a body of men who enjoyed robust good health, I was not even sure what my responsibilities were as a medical man towards Holmes. Viewed objectively, he was no more than someone I shared quarters with. Yet each night after the fit had been upon him, my conscience swelled within me at the thought that I lacked the courage to protest at his habit of injecting himself thrice or more per day and I determined that I should deliver my soul upon the subject the very next day. But there was that cool, nonchalant air of my companion which made him the last man with whom one would care to take anything approaching a liberty. His great powers, his masterly manner, and the experience which I had had of his many extraordinary qualities, all made me diffident and backward in crossing him.

And yet in my domestic darkness, there was something to look forward to.

I had taken a future position on some South American stocks which I had been assured by my billiard-playing friend and some-time investment advisor, Thurston, were a one-way bet to rise. The settlement date for the shares was the 30th of August. My contract had been to pay my stockbroker, Mr Arthur Courcy, for the shares at the 16th of August price with the intention of selling them immediately at the higher price that Thurston was as sure as his word would obtain by the end of August. For my part, I was sure I would be able to find a way of bridging the gap between when I would have to pay for the shares and the much larger amount I would not receive until a slightly later date. "I cannot give you investment advice, Dr Watson," said the strongly built Courcy gravely. "The value of shares can go down as well as up and with this investment you do not even have past performance as a guide. I am the true risk taker as, alas, I am with so many of the investments of my more adventurous clients. Although," he added as afterthought, "I am used to recovering monies owed to me and take every necessary measure to do so."

Yet there stood the listing of Bogotá Property Holdings in the financial press! And, as Thurston had forecast, they stood at a price well above what I was contracted to pay and only a catastrophic fall in their value could prevent me making a handsome and most welcome profit on them.

I visited the England players at their hotel to find them in good spirits.

Hornby had gained the sobriquet "Monkey" because of his restless verve which gave him the energy to captain England not only at cricket but also at rugby. As I had been on my return to England, he was as brown as a nut, but in his case his tan came from spending much time outdoors even though the summer had been a rainy one making the carrying of an umbrella wherever one went unavoidable. "It is good to see you, Dr Watson," he said. "We are practising at the Oval tomorrow. We would like you to be in attendance in case any of our team suffers from any niggles. They have had long train journeys from every corner of the country and some of them may have a reaction tomorrow.

That's the life of a modern cricketer. Travel, practise, play. Travel, practise, play. We will be at the ground from ten o'clock and the Australian boys will be there as well. We will have one side of the ground, and they'll have the other."

When I returned to Baker Street, it was to find Holmes in an extreme state of exhilaration.

In *The Dying Detective*, my friend feigned delirium by babbling about oysters, batteries, and the weight of coins in small change. On that August evening in 1882 muscle development, gun emplacements, and the part mint can play in loss of weight were the subjects of his ravings, and I found listening to my friend's incoherent maunderings on these subjects no less difficult than when a few years later I found him, as I thought, on the verge of death from a tropical illness. In this earlier episode his ravings were unfeigned, and it took many hours before he came to his senses. I ended up sitting up with him on the other side of the hearth into the small hours, and he only stopped with his wild and rambling discourses as the sky turned from deep black to an iron grey heralding the break of dawn. I nodded off and sat up with a start at half past seven. Holmes woke shortly afterwards looking as grey as the heavy rain clouds that had gathered outside.

"I fear I have rather over-reached myself," his normally incisive voice reduced to a hoarse, uncertain whisper. It says much that rather than seeking comfort in tobacco, coffee, or – heaven preserve us – yet another injection of cocaine, he confined himself to sipping a glass of water which wobbled precariously in his hand as he raised it to his lips. I felt I could not leave my friend on his own, but I still had my duties – for which I was being paid, and how I still needed the money! – at the Oval. In the end I said, at my wit's end, "Holmes, I am contracted to the English cricket team, and I must go to the Oval this morning. If you can dress, you may come with me. I will present you to Mr Hornby as a mature medical student who is shadowing me to gain experience. I must beg you to confine yourself to healthy stimulants such as tobacco or snuff and abjure anything injurious like cocaine."

This was as close as I ever got to giving Holmes an instruction and I suspect that under any other circumstances it would have resulted in a flat refusal or even a breach in what was then at most an incipient friendship. As it was, Holmes nodded absently before rising unsteadily to his feet and going to his room to ready himself for the day.

As we walked down to Baker Street Station, to my surprise, Holmes asked me for an explanation of cricket. Given that I had already formed the view that my new friend's knowledge of most matters apart from crime was nil, I thought I had better start at the fundamentals.

"Cricket," I began, "is played between two teams of eleven players. One side equipped with a ball takes all eleven of its members onto the field and they are called the fielding side. The other side called the batting side is represented by two players who take the field with the objective of scoring points or runs as they are referred to."

"Why are they referred to as runs?"

"Each batsman defends a target called a wicket from a ball propelled by a member of the fielding side called a bowler. The batting team tries to strike the ball out of the reach of the fielding side in such a way as to give the two batsmen enough time to run between the two wickets. Each time they do so, the batting side scores a so-called run."

"And what does the fielding side do?"

"They try to bowl the ball in such a way as to make it difficult to strike the ball and with the objective of making the batsman commit an infraction such as missing the ball so that it strikes the wicket, or having the ball caught directly from the bat. Sometimes the batsmen attempt to run between the wickets and do not complete the distance they are required to run before the fielding side breaks the wicket with the ball."

"What is the distance the batsmen is required to run?"

"The two wickets are twenty-two yards apart and a yard in front of each wicket is a line. To complete a run, the batsman must be across the line before the wicket is broken. The distance they run is therefore twenty yards."

"What happens if one of these infractions, as you put it, occurs?"

"If the batsman has his wicket struck, or if the ball is caught off the bat without touching the turf, or if the batsman fails to complete a run before the wicket is broken – the batsman is replaced by one of his teammates and that continues until all the players on the first team have batted. Once that has happened, the other team goes in to bat and seeks to exceed the tally of runs made by the first team which is now in the field. The team that scores the most runs and dismisses all the batsmen of its opponents wins the game. It is a game which combines strategy, skill, courage, concentration, and luck. In a lesser game where taking part is as important as winning, each side bats once but in a big game such as the one coming up between the English and Australian teams, each eleven bats twice."

"You make yourself very plain."

And with these words, to my considerable surprise, my friend turned round and ran back up Baker Street towards 221. I was uncertain as to what to do as I did not wish to leave him on his own but also did not want to be late at the Oval but, to my relief, I had gone back no more a couple of hundred paces when my friend reappeared unchanged apart from an overcoat – not an unwise precaution even though the sun was showing signs of breaking through. I was myself wearing thick clothes and was armed with the inevitable umbrella as well as my medical bag. Sticking out of Holmes's coat pocket I could see a protractor, a set of dividers, and a bulky notebook which made him look like a carpenter.

"Now I am quite ready," said he, and lit his pipe. I noted on his countenance the glazed expression which he adopted for his moments of deepest contemplation, and he retained this look throughout the journey from Baker Street Station to Vauxhall via Victoria. He was not to speak again until we were crossing the Oval's now sun-dappled greensward. On either side of the ground, three strips of grass had been mown close and rolled and netting set up over them so that the players – the English or our left and the Australians on our right – could practise without the ball going far from where it had been hit.

"I'll introduce you to the England captain, Mr Hornby," I said to Holmes. "The captain of the Australians is over there. He is called William Murdoch."

"I take it," replied Holmes, "that the role of the captain is to identify the weakness of each batsman on the opposing side and to make sure the bowler is briefed to aim the ball in such a way as to exploit that weakness. And he must place his fields..."

But before he could continue, Hornby had made his way over to us. He was padded and gloved ready to go into the nets for his own batting practice. I made introductions and then asked him if he had any special concerns about his players.

"George Ulyett," he said,

– "He is the fastest bowler in England and also a good batsman," I explained to Holmes –

"has come up sore in the back this morning. Could you go and have a look at him in the dressing room, Doctor? I am not aware of any other problems, but you had probably best ask the other players if they have any concerns as they come in and out."

Holmes and I were soon in the England dressing room where Ulyett, was laid up.

"I think I sat awkwardly on the train on the way down south from Yorkshire, Doctor," he said. "It's not enough to stop me bowling but it will stop me bowling flat out."

I asked him to lie face down on the treatment table and he pulled his shirt up so that I could look at the affected area. Under my fingers I could feel the tautness of the muscles on the left side of his spine, and I started to knead them using an unguent of my own preparation. I was so engrossed in my work, that it was quite a few minutes before I looked around and saw that Holmes had disappeared. Ulyett raised his head from the table and said, "I can see your colleague. He is out on the field." The famous cricketer paused. "He is sitting so still, he looks in a kind of trance. And he's got something pointed in his hand."

I feared the worst and, abandoning my work, I went back onto the field, hard pressed not to break into a run.

As Ulyett had said, my friend was sitting on the grass, but it was only when I approached him that I could see he was alternately looking through the pair of dividers and writing intently in his notebook as he watched, as though beguiled, the England team at its practice. He did not stir as I approached, and it was only when I crossed his eyeline that he gave any sign of being aware that I was there.

"I am checking," he said, "the best angle to bowl the ball at each player and at which point before the batsman to land it."

"You mean the line and length."

"Look at the large man with the beard over there," said Holmes, not responding.

"Dr WG Grace, England's best batsman."

"He is a doctor as well as a cricketer?"

"That is so."

Holmes paused to consider this and then continued.

"Very good then, he is clearly a man of multiple talents. And as a cricketer, in spite of his girth, Grace has a range of shots far beyond that of any other player, so a tight line and an accurate length are required to keep him quiet. If a bowler can manage that, Grace will get impatient and commit an infraction of the type you described."

"You mean he will be dismissed and have to be replaced by another batsman?" I responded to make sure I had understood what Holmes had said.

But my friend was apparently too taken by the game to respond to my comments. "Here in cricket, there are possibilities indeed for the scientific observer. I have been dim not to notice them before. The man over there…" he nodded at a man I knew to be Richard Barlow, England's stonewalling opening batsman and key bowler, "has an almost impenetrable defence but no attacking shots so one can bowl loosely at him and not fear punishment."

As though seeking to confirm my friend's assessment, Barlow prodded at the next two balls so that they dropped at his feet, but by now Holmes was already looking for a new challenge as he had already wheeled away to look at the Australian players.

"Murdoch is tall and so is adept at putting his left leg down the pitch and hitting the ball straight," said Holmes staring at the Australian captain and paying no heed to me.

"Murdoch is the best Australian batsman," I murmured.

"How do you know that?" asked Holmes, responding directly to one of my remarks for the first time in a while. "Even as a user of scientific reasoning, I would be reluctant to express so definitive an opinion based on mere observation of a few deliveries to him."

"I am sure that statistics can substantiate it."

"What sort of statistics are there about cricket?"

"Oh," I said airily, "if you are keen on such things, you can get the average number of runs each batsman makes each inning before he is dismissed, and the average number of runs a bowler concedes between taking wickets. You can also find out how many catches each man has taken. For the true enthusiast, the list is almost without end."

"I thought the skills of deduction, observation and analysis could only be applied to criminal investigation, but here I find an activity that lends itself to my skills just as well."

I was intrigued at Holmes's interest in a sport that he had seemed to know nothing about only a short time before but now a tall, moustached figure with saturnine features strode down the steps of the pavilion and out onto the field.

"That's Fred Spofforth, Australia's best bowler," I commented. "His looks and skills have earned him the nickname the Demon."

Holmes and I watched as Spofforth marked a short run up and ambled up to bowl. If my friend's attention had been engaged by watching the English players, he became positively animated as he watched Spofforth. "In this man I see a kindred spirit. He has intuition and precision. The short stature of the batsman – "

"Blackham, the Australian wicket-keeper, though he is also a useful batsman," I advised.

"– and the fact that he is standing a little way back from the direct line between the wickets indicates Blackham likes to play slashing shots away from his body. Spofforth is keeping the ball wide of the wicket to tempt the batsman but not wide enough to make the shot a risk free one."

As we watched, the slight Blackham took a step back to essay a cut at a ball that was a little too straight for the shot and the ball went off the inside edge and rolled into the stumps.

"Spofforth's method is very simple, and effective," mused Holmes. "He is accurate and can target any imperfection in the turf to make the ball deviate. But I would have thought that he would bowl more quickly than he does if he has a nickname like the Demon for he is no quicker than the fastest of the other bowlers who are practising here."

"I understand that he is capable of bowling very fast, but you are right to say he looks quite gentle today. Maybe he is carrying an injury and trying to keep loose."

"And what does a wicketkeeper, as you have described Blackham as being, do?"

"He collects the ball behind the wicket if it passes the batsman after the bowler has bowled it and from the fieldsmen when they throw the ball in after it has been struck."

I felt that if Holmes, completely contrary to my expectations, was so taken by cricket, it was safe to leave him on the field, and I returned to my medical duties.

By mid-afternoon I had done all that could be done for the players, and Holmes and I returned to Baker Street. To my relief, and I confess slightly to my surprise, Holmes, rather than reaching for the syringe, pulled out from his copious archives all the newspapers he could lay his hands on, and spent the evening poring over the sports pages and laboriously filling his notebook with column after column of figures. I stayed up late thinking that my presence in our sitting room might discourage my friend from succumbing to the temptation to reach for the syringe, but I need not have feared as my fellow-lodger was completely engrossed by his work. When I eventually departed to bed, guttering candle in hand, he looked up from his activity, a look of seraphic tranquillity on his face, and remarked, "I can think of nothing better than cricket to hone my abilities in scientific reasoning. I do not know when I shall retire."

I rose late the next morning and found the sitting-room deserted.

"I heard Mr Holmes leave the house early, Dr Watson," said Mrs Hudson in response to my question of the whereabouts of my friend when she brought me my breakfast.

"Did he say where he was going?" I asked, fearing the worst, and completely unsurprised when our landlady knew nothing. But at six in the evening he returned, the look of tranquillity still on his countenance and a bulky primrose yellow volume, which I knew to be that bible of cricket, *Wisden Cricketers' Almanac*, in his hand.

"I have spent the day studying cricket at the local library where there is a broad range of books on techniques and statistics, and I will continue now to remedy the deficiency in my knowledge of it," said he. "Cricket offers the most complex of human dramas combining psychology and physiognomy". He was to pass the rest of the evening and all the next day studying his new fascination and addressed not a word to me.

The All England versus Australia match was scheduled to last three days. My contract stated I needed to be at the ground throughout and Holmes insisted on joining me for the first day. With his new obsession, my friend was changed out of all recognition from the drug-addled wreck of but a few days before. His first move on emerging from our quarters in Baker Street was to buy a copy of each newspaper and he dedicated himself to studying the sports pages of these on our way to the Oval. As an associate of the England team, we were able to enter the ground without having to queue with the rest of the vast crowd – 20,000 strong, we learned later – and I had been given two complimentary seats within hailing distance of the England dressing-room as I was only required to be inside it when called for.

As soon as we had taken our seats, Holmes fished his notebook out of his pocket, glanced down a long page of figures and commented, "The batting average of each member of the Australian team this season is in each case below that of his English counterpart. One would thus expect the English to outscore their Australian counterparts. And the two main English bowlers, Peate and Barlow both have lower bowling averages than even the demonic Mr Spofforth and Boyle, Australia's other main bowler. Accordingly, England ought to win this at a canter."

"Cricket is a game of many twists. You cannot just go on averages."

England bowled the Australians out for only sixty-three with Blackham and Murdoch making the top scores while Holmes grumbled that England bowled too wide to the former and too full to the latter. England were bowled out themselves for one-hundred-and-one with Spofforth taking seven wickets although his speed never lived up to the demonic nickname, and the wicket-keeper, Blackham, stood up to the stumps, and affected what I knew to be a stumping.

Holmes needed an explanation of what this was, and I explained, "While the ball is in play – so roughly from the time the ball leaves to bowler's hand to when it is returned to him to bowl the next ball, the batsman must stay within his ground – that is to say, behind the line that he must cross to complete a run. If he ventures out of it for any reason, and the fielding side, normally the wicket-keeper, breaks the stumps with the ball, the batsman is deemed to be dismissed."

Holmes nodded and then said, "I am not sure that Spofforth bowling at a speed that enables Blackham to stand directly behind the stumps is a sensible tactic even if he pulls off an occasional stumping when the batsman is out of his ground. Spofforth would be quite twice as effective if he bowled at a speed justifying his nickname of the Demon."

But by the end of play, Holmes was looking delighted. "My model using averages has worked as a perfect predictor of the outcome of today. The batting averages of the England players this season spread across eleven players should give England an average score of 316 while the Australian average over the same period is 227."

"But both sides have fallen well short of those totals – "

"The absolute score will be influenced by playing conditions – the condition of the pitch, how close the outfield has been cut, and so on. If it has been wet, as it has here, scores will be lower as the pitch will cut up and so not be even. It is the ratio between the teams' performance that is key to the performance of the teams. The ratio of the England average to the Australian one, so between 316 and 227, is 1.37 so you would expect England's innings to conclude at 1.37 times that of the Australian one."

We were already on the road to Vauxhall station when he said this, and I felt I had to puncture Holmes's pride at reducing a sport to a mathematical model by pointing out, "But England's score is over one and a half times the Australian score –"

"In fact 1.60 times," corrected my friend.

"– so, have England not over-performed based on your model? If Australia scored sixty-three, should England not have been contained to..." and I paused as multiplying 1.37 by sixty-three was a little beyond my mathematical prowess -

"Eighty-six," chipped in Holmes, as I wondered if I had enough fingers to make the calculations. "But, he went on, "you are failing to take account of the relative strength of the two bowlers. Boyle and Spofforth take wickets at an average 1.17 times the average for Peate and Barlow, England's main bowlers. Once you factor that in, the ratio between the England score and the Australian score should be 1.63. Thus, the actual outcome that the England score is 1.60 times the Australian one is within 2% of the expected one and so well within the parameters of statistical error."

But I was no longer listening for, on the street-side newsstand with the evening papers, my eye had caught a headline saying, "Massive Earthquake in Colombia." When I picked up the paper, it was to learn that the earthquake was centred on Bogotá and the ground on which the city stood had cracked to the extent that many of its buildings had disappeared into the crevices. I suppose that my concern should really have been about Bogotá's stricken inhabitants, but instead I turned feverishly to the financial pages where I saw that the share price of Bogotá Property Holdings had gone the same way as the city's buildings and so, rather than collecting a handsome profit when my contract matured, I was faced by a loss that I had no means of covering.

I confided my predicament to my friend who appeared to listen for a while without saying anything and soon switched into expatiating on his new sporting passion which he continued to do all the way back to Baker Street. I was too preoccupied to make any remark of my own and retired early to bed where I spent a sleepless night as I turned over in my head my options.

On the next day I was minded not to go the Oval at all, but my friend's face fell when I suggested I might send my apologies, and we set off for the ground. It was raining heavily, and I commented to Holmes, "They will not be able to start on time."

"And when they do, the turf will be soft and cut up, so batting will be difficult," was his reply.

As a precaution, I went to the bank on the way to the station and took out all the cash I was able to muster as I wanted to make sure I could at least meet my rental payment due on the first of the month, the coming Friday, before my stockbroker distrained my assets. Even then I only had three quarters of the amount needed to pay Mrs Hudson, and I dreaded even thinking about how I might explain my embarrassment to her, and dreaded even more having to find a dwelling even less prepossessing than the one I currently occupied or, even worse, being incarcerated in a debtors' prison.

On our arrival at Oval, I sought out Hornby and he requested that I look at Steel, who had a swollen ankle. Holmes, Steel, and I were in one corner of the changing room as I strapped Steel up. This took longer than I expected, and I am not sure whether Hornby was aware of our presence as he gave a short speech to his team before the start of play. "Boys," he said, "we represent our country, and we have a fight on our hands against the Colonials. Let us get out there and not give them an inch."

Holmes and I took our normal seats as Australia went into bat and tried to make up their deficit on the first innings.

By contrast with my nervous state, Holmes seemed in the best of humours.

"Why does Hornby not give Ulyett a longer spell against Massie," he opined as the Australian opening batsman's score mounted. "Ulyett got him quickly in the first innings."

Maybe it was desperation, but a thought now struck me.

Given Holmes's certainty, backed by impressive statistical research, that the Englishman had the better side, should I use the last money I had on a bet?

I went round to the betting tent where odds of three to one on or, as our American cousins would say one to three, were being offered for England. Thus, if I bet the nine pounds I had in my pocket, and England won, I would make three pounds, which added to my stake would make twelve pounds. That would give me enough to pay my rent for the month ahead even though this was represented only a sixth of my exposure to the cost of buying the shares of Bogotá Property Holdings at the 14th of August price. I was torn. And then, as I stood at the stand, a roar from the crowd signalled the dismissal of Australia's Massie and even as I watched the odds chalked up on the board were reduced to from three to one to seven to two on meaning my nine pounds would only yield eleven pounds eight shillings and six pence.

I went back to my seat and watched as more wickets fell but then Murdoch and Blackham started a stand which, I could only assume, would cause the odds on an England to win to move to my advantage. In the end I was so unsure of myself that I asked Holmes what I should do.

"None of the factors about the team that I have enumerated to you have changed," was all that he would say, not taking his eyes from the game in front of us.

If I already felt too nervous for thought before, my reader may imagine my horror when I now saw two rows in front of me and to my right, my stockbroker, Mr Courcy. Was he here just to watch the cricket or was he shadowing me to see what assets he could prise from me when I failed to meet my debt for the Bogotá Property Holdings shares? Or was he even aware of my impending insolvency? I noted he seemed to be in a party of men notable for their burliness and I wondered whether that was how he enforced his contracts with insolvent investors.

I did not want to draw attention to myself and so was reluctant to rise from my seat again. In the end I was reduced to asking Holmes in a low whisper to go and place it for me on condition that he could secure odds on England of three to one on or better. Inevitably as soon as my friend went off to place the bet, Blackham fell which was likely to make the odds even worse.

Shortly afterwards occurred an incident which continues to divide opinion among followers of the noble game.

The Australian number nine, Jones, completed a run and then went out of his ground to pat down a divot on the still wet pitch. Dr Grace, ball in hand, broke the wicket. There was no doubt that the ball was in play and no doubt that Jones was out by the laws of the game, but there was also no doubt that Jones had not been seeking to take a run or to gain any other sort of advantage. Discussion in the crowd ranged from comments that Jones would eventually thank Grace for teaching him a lesson to demands that the England captain ask the umpire for Jones to be recalled as Grace had behaved unsportingly. For his own part, Jones stormed off the field.

The next man in was the tall Spofforth and even from the crowd, we could hear angry words being exchanged by the players with Spofforth saying to Grace, "That piece of poor sportsmanship is all you'll ever be remembered for." For his part Grace could be heard advising Spofforth to make a study of the game's laws.

And where was Holmes? Had he been able to place my bet at odds of three to one on? Would I be able to pay my rent for September? And how would I pay for the collapse in the price of Bogotá Property Holdings? My friend did not return, and I could not risk rising from my seat for fear of attracting the attention of Mr Courcy and his burly and to my eyes somewhat rough-looking associates. As it was, the cricket boiled up in a cauldron of excitement as the dismissal of the last Australian batsman left England with eighty-five to win.

The umpires came out onto the field for the final innings of the game followed by the Australian players. As they came, I could hear Spofforth exhorting his team-mates, "Come on boys, this thing can be done!" Finally, the England opening batsmen, Grace and Hornby, emerged and battle was joined. And what a battle! It was obvious to me that Spofforth was fired up. He sprinted in from fully twenty yards and wicket-keeper Blackham, now standing twenty yards behind the wicket at the other end, had to leap like a jack-in-the-box to take the ball as it flew past the batsman. First Hornby and then England number three, Barlow, were bowled by Spofforth, and, rather than the ball rolling onto the wicket as had happened when Spofforth had bowled Blackham at practice, the stumps reacted as if detonated when the ball struck them and were sent flying out of the ground.

Nevertheless, England reached forty for only two men down and so were only forty-five runs from victory. The feeling came over me that my money and my good name were safe at least for now. As though to confirm the point, Dr Grace on two separate occasions struck the ball with such force that it pierced the field and ran to the rope that separates the playing area from the spectators. Had my friend been there, I would have explained that this meant the batsman scored four runs without having run the distance between the wickets. These two strikes closed the distance to victory to a mere thirty-four runs. It was at this point that I saw Australia's captain leave the field, although he returned a couple of minutes later. I noted that when he did so, he immediately set the field slightly further back making it harder to get the ball to the boundary and Dr Grace was too portly to take fast singles to the deeper set fieldsmen.

Time seemed to stand still as Spofforth and Boyle sent down ball after ball which Grace and Ulyett, his partner, seemed unable to get away. Then Spofforth got Ulyett and straight afterwards Grace fell to Boyle. At the fall of each wicket, I noticed Murdoch once more sprint off the field although he always came straight back. I wondered if he had a stomach ailment but whatever was troubling him, he seemed to have a specific plan for each remaining England batsman. Every time one of them struck the ball, it seemed to go to a fieldman, and the Australians bowled, caught, intercepted, and threw the ball to the wicket-keeper like men possessed. I noticed Courcy took to chewing on the handle of his umbrella though whether it was the state of the cricket or the state of my finances that made him adopt this method of handling his nerves, I could not be sure. Soon Boyle shattered the stumps of Peate, England's last man, and England had lost by seven runs. I saw Courcy stand up, the handle of his umbrella chewed into two pieces, but that was the last I saw of him as the disappointed crowd rose and came between us and I took pains not to look in his direction.

It then struck me that although my contract with the England cricket team was at an end just as my life as a free and solvent man seemed to be, I still had an honorarium owing for my services as the team doctor of the English team, and I went to the changing-room to collect it even although I knew I would probably soon be handing it over to bailiffs.

As my reader may imagine, the mood in the changing-room was as despondent as my own. I was slightly surprised to find Holmes already there who said to me, "When I came back to our seats, you had gone, but I knew you would have to come here."

"Where have you been?" I asked but, before Holmes could answer, Hornby came over to us. "I will pay you for your services in this game, Dr Watson, but I fear I will not be able to employ you again. I have been told that your associate Mr Holmes was seen in a betting tent. Intimate involvement in the game and gambling do not go together."

"But he was placing a bet on my behalf on England," I protested. "I had every confidence we would win, and I placed my stake accordingly."

"I fear cricket is not called for nothing the noble game and whether it was your bet or that of your associate and regardless of what side you were betting on, gambling was inappropriate for someone so closely linked to the team. I shall report your actions to the cricket authorities who will doubtless ban you and your associate from any further involvement with our sport. Here is your cheque. We have met our obligations. It is a shame that you did not meet yours. I consider the matter closed, and have nothing further to say to you."

Holmes and I made a gloomy way towards the station. "I was able to get odds for you of..." began my friend.

..."What the deuce does it matter what the odds were that you got me," I interrupted bitterly, "when my stake was placed on the wrong result?"

"I was about to say I was able to get you odds of seven to one against an Australian win. The bookmakers increased the odds against it when Jones got out, but I was sure that, angered by Grace's action in running out Jones and Grace's response to Spofforth's protests, Spofforth would bowl at full speed. I thought a full-speed Spofforth would average half his average for the first innings when he took seven wickets for forty-six runs and if Boyle performed at the same level, then I estimated Australia would bowl England out for seventy-six and the fact that England got to seventy-seven is an acceptable statistical error."

"You placed the stake which represented my entire fortune on Australia when I had asked you to place it on England?" I asked wondering whether I was hearing correctly.

"I knew that an England win would only cover your rent for one month and when Grace did what he did to Jones, I thought Australia at seven to one against represented good value. And so it has proved."

"But that was pure speculation on your part."

"Not at all. The result was the product of my reasoning and statistical analysis. But I also needed to factor in the effect of Spofforth's anger as cricket is a game of psychology as well as numbers."

"So where were you when England was batting?"

"I had handed a note into the Australian dressing-room saying that I could give them a method to dismiss each England batsman for a minimal score. Murdoch was unconvinced but he still asked me into the dressing-room. When he could not part Ulyett and Dr Grace as they added thirty-six, he decided to avail himself of my services. Once he had taken my advice of setting the field back so that Grace could not make up for his inability to run singles by piercing the field for boundaries, Grace fell, and Murdoch became convinced of my method."

"So that was why he left the field at the fall of each wicket. He was consulting with you."

"Yes, that is so. Each time a new batsman appeared, Murdoch would ask me for a plan for him. He implemented it and, after Grace had gone, I was able to ensure that no batsman got more than twelve runs."

"And I have enough money to cover the liability for my shares."

"That is also so."

Two days later I received a letter from the Marylebone Cricket Club which imposed a ban on Holmes and me from any involvement with cricket *sine die*. Contrary to the quotation from *Tom Brown's School Days* which heads this account of events, there was no suggestion of trial by jury let alone of an appeal. I was merely relieved that I was not under arrest and not having to rely on *habeas corpus* to have any chance of getting out. I was thus able to view the ban with more equanimity than might otherwise have been the case. By contrast Holme was incensed.

"I would be happy if they knew my methods and would be free to apply them for themselves!" he expostulated. "Like the master in *Tom Brown's School Days*, I understood the game scientifically. And the bet I placed was not even on my own behalf."

I suspect that if Holmes had not been banned from any involvement in cricket, he might have made his living on the earnings he would have made as a gambler on cricket with insights from statistics no one else could manage. Indeed, I suggested this to him as a means of occupying himself in these early days when his practice was minimal. His response was to shrug and say, "The insights on cricket I have shared with you thus far are a mixture of statistical analysis and observation of cricket in action. One cannot profitably make use of the former without access to the latter and I will have no access to the latter as I am banned from every cricket ground in the country. I will now seek to forget everything I have learnt about it."

His reaction to his ban from cricket was to succumb once more to the needle and that explains the long span – much longer than the so-called Great Hiatus of 1891 to 1894 – between the time we started sharing quarters together and our first dated collaboration of 1887 although my readers will realize that some of the early cases do not bear a date. In that harrowing period, time often seemed to stand still as I ministered to my friend, his body distended and the pupils of his eye reduced to pinholes by his misuse of drugs. I confess I might have been less willing to perform this service to him had not his betting coup saved my good name. I noted that sometimes in his delirium he would, to express his sense of loss at his ban from cricket, quote that wistful poem about time and death which started this narrative as he thought back to the pleasure cricket had given him, – "Oh my Hornby and my Barlow long ago, long ago".

Note by Henry Durham, historical advisor to *The Redacted Sherlock Holmes* series

The 1882 match Dr Watson describes is the encounter between the Australian tourists and an eleven described at the time as All England but now regarded as being a representative England team. Afterwards *The Sporting Times* published a mock obituary of English cricket and stated that its body would be cremated, and its ashes taken to Australia. Cricketing encounters between England and Australia are still described as being a contest for The Ashes.

This is the first time that the presence of Dr Watson and Sherlock Holmes at the game and the role of the latter in Australia's victory have been disclosed. Dr Watson's recollection of events and scores is remarkably accurate, and having consulted numerous sources of information on the match, I have had to change nothing in his account. Readers wanting a more detailed version of events may like to look at the account of the match in the Wisden of 1883 where they will find further statistical analysis. The statistics used are described as being the work of a Mr Henry Luff, but such is the detail of the numbers provided, it is hard to imagine that this analysis was not the work of Sherlock Holmes.

The masticatory destruction of his own umbrella by stockbroker, Mr Arthur Courcy, was the subject of many reports at the time but this is the first occasion that the suggestion has been made that Courcy may have been more concerned by the recoverability of speculative debts relating to Bogotá Property Holdings than by the cricket.

Printed in the USA
CPSIA information can be obtained
at www.ICGtesting.com
LVHW052340141024
793784LV00033B/475